P9-DJB-132

HEAD FOR COVER!

Toward morning the wind picked up until it was near hurricane force, buffeting the wagons and violently shaking the canvas covers. Nate was constantly on the lookout for a suitable place where the settlers could make their stand. Finally, on a ridge, he was overjoyed to find a small spring sheltered by boulders just below the crest. With the vegetation burned away, there were few places the hostiles could take advantage of.

"This will have to do," Nate said, moving along the rim. Nodding in satisfaction, he moved to the west side and rose in the saddle to beckon the emigrants to join him. But as he raised his arm, he paused.

To the south, advancing at a determined dogtrot, was a long line of figures.

The Piegan braves were coming and they would be out for blood.

The *Wilderness* series published by *Leisure Books:*

11

WILDERNESS

Northwest Passage

David Thompson

LEISURE BOOKS   NEW YORK CITY

Dedicated to Judy, Joshua, and Shane.
And to Nathaniel Hawthorne, who exposed it first.

A LEISURE BOOK®

October 1992

Published by

Dorchester Publishing Co., Inc.
276 Fifth Avenue
New York, NY 10001

If you purchased this book without a cover you should be aware that this book is stolen property. It was reported as "unsold and destroyed" to the publisher and neither the author nor the publisher has received any payment for this "stripped book."

Copyright © 1992 by David L. Robbins

All rights reserved. No part of this book may be reproduced or transmitted in any form or by any electronic or mechanical means, including photocopying, recording or by any information storage and retrieval system, without the written permission of the Publisher, except where permitted by law.

The name "Leisure Books" and the stylized "L" with design are trademarks of Dorchester Publishing Co., Inc.

Printed in the United States of America.

Chapter One

The piercing scream cut through the hot Plains air like a razor-sharp butcher knife through buffalo fat.

On one knee at the base of a low knoll, Nathaniel King tensed and glanced up from the fresh elk tracks he had been examining. The scream wavered eerily on a gust of wind. Before the last lingering notes died, Nate took three strides and vaulted onto his magnificent pied stallion. A tug on the reins and a jab of his moccasins brought the horse to an immediate gallop, and he raced off across the prairie toward the spot where he had left the pilgrims from the States.

Nate's first thought was that his greenhorn charges were under attack by hostiles, perhaps by a wandering band of Sioux, Arapaho, or even Blackfeet. There had been no sign of marauding war parties in the area, but a man could never be certain where Indians were concerned; they were as crafty as coyotes, as invisible as ghosts.

He clasped his Hawken firmly in his right hand and focused on the stand of trees sheltering the three wagons from the scorching sun. Oddly, he saw no hint of a commotion, and there should be a swirl of violent activity if a war party had struck. Not until he was 50 yards away did he see moving figures under the trees, some of them wildly waving their arms, and hear angry yells. Another 20 yards showed him the reason for the alarm.

A black bear was trying to clamber into one of the wagons.

Nate slowed and almost laughed aloud at the comical sight of the settlers prancing and dancing around the oblivious bear. It had its front paws braced on the side of the rear freight wagon, and was bobbing its big head up and down in the typical way a bear did when testing a breeze for scent. In this instance, it had no doubt been drawn to the wagons by the tantalizing odors coming from the food and other supplies piled high inside.

Black bears were seldom dangerous. A female with cubs would attack anyone foolhardy enough to approach too close, and a cornered bear was always likely to charge, but ordinarily they avoided humans like the plague. Unlike their fierce cousins, the mighty grizzlies, black bears possessed a mild temperament.

So Nate was not particularly concerned until he spied one of the Banner party, young Harry Nesmith, take aim with a rifle. "No!" he bellowed, and sped forward, seeking to avert potential calamity.

The rifle, a .50-caliber Kentucky, boomed.

Any hope of driving the hungry bear off without any trouble was dashed as the enraged creature dropped onto all fours and whirled, its gaping mouth wide in a vicious roar. It glared at the humans standing nearby, then abruptly charged a thin woman who stood immobilized with fear.

Nate was nearly there. Letting go of the reins, he used his legs to guide the stallion as he whipped the Hawken to his right shoulder, cocked the hammer, and took a hasty bead on the bear's head. Going for the heart or the lungs was unwise since a single ball in either often failed to bring a bear down. But the head shot, even if not fatal, might stun the black bear long enough for Nate to finish the unfortunate beast off.

The furious bear had only two yards to cover to reach the terrified woman when the Hawken cracked. In a whirl of limbs the brute went down, rolling completely over and smacking into the transfixed pilgrim. She flew to one side, landing on her back. The black bear was upright in the blink of an eye, snarling as it shook its head from side to side.

A heartbeat after squeezing the trigger, Nate was already grabbing for another weapon. His right hand streaked to one of the two smoothbore single-shot .55-caliber flintlock pistols wedged under his wide brown leather belt, and as the stallion came abreast of the bear he leaned down, lowered the barrel to within an inch of the bear's brow, and fired.

The black bear's head snapped to one side as if kicked by a Missouri mule. Then the bear blinked, tried to lift a paw, and sagged, its front legs buckling first. Snorting and spitting blood, it went prone.

Nate turned the stallion in a tight loop and leaped down before the horse came to a stop. Transferring the spent flintlock to the same hand that held the Hawken, he drew his other pistol, dashed up to the wheezing bear, which was struggling to rise, and dispatched it with a ball between the eyes. For a full ten seconds he stood still, inhaling the acrid gunsmoke, watching blood flow from the bear's wounds.

"Well done, King! I don't understand why my shot didn't do the trick."

The lighthearted words aroused Nate's anger. He spun, his features hardening, and strode up to Harry Nesmith. "Damn your hide!" he snapped, jabbing the flintlock into Nesmith's chest. The startled Ohioan stumbled backwards. "You had no call to go and shoot! We could have driven the critter off."

"Why are you so mad?" Nesmith responded indignantly. "We couldn't let that beast get into our victuals."

"Yes, King," interjected a deep voice to their right. "Why are you so upset?"

Nate shifted to face the leader of the group, Simon Banner. A tall, powerful blockhouse of a man who wore homespun clothes and a white hat, Banner constantly exuded a certain arrogance that rankled Nate no end. "Out here, Mr. Banner," he answered slowly, keeping his tone calm and level with a supreme effort, "we don't kill anything unless we absolutely have to. We don't ever waste game." He nodded at the dead black bear. "There was no need to kill it."

Banner scratched his bearded chin, then shrugged. "I still don't see what the fuss is all about. It's just a bear. We kill them all the time back East."

"Which is why there are fewer and fewer bears every year," Nate stated flatly. "You're not east of the Mississippi any longer, and it's time you owned up to that fact." He encompassed the prairie with a sweep of his arm. "Out here we do things differently. You might say we do as the Indians do. And Indians never kill animals unless they need those animals for food or their lives are in peril."

Banner made a sniffing sound. "We've only been together for a week, yet I can tell you admire the savages more than they rightfully deserve. They are heathens, after all."

It took all the self-control Nate could muster not to smash Banner on the mouth. "Need I remind you that my wife is a Shoshoni?" he asked gruffly.

"She is?" Banner replied in genuine surprise. "My word, King. I wasn't told."

For a moment Nate was inclined to doubt the assertion, until he reminded himself that the man who had arranged for him to serve as guide for this bunch, Isaac Fraeb, was a tight-lipped old cuss who never indulged in idle gossip. "Well, now you have been," he said. "So I'll thank you not to speak ill of the Indians again in my presence or I'll be obliged to show you better manners."

He sighed, his temper subsiding, aware that many Easterners shared Banner's prejudice through no fault of their own. When the government itself regarded Indians as little better than animals, it was only natural for those who believed in their government to feel the same way. Very few knew the truth. Very few had experienced what he had experienced. "Not all Indians are as bad as they're painted to be," he commented. "Some are as friendly as any white man who ever lived. And most are honest, upright people in their own way."

"How can heathens be upright in the sight of the Lord?" Banner asked quizzically. "Isn't that a contradiction in terms?"

"I suppose *you* would say so," Nate said. The man was, after all, the brother-in-law of a Methodist missionary, and as devout as a Quaker.

Suddenly a shrill reprimand was addressed at them both. "Isn't this a fine state of affairs? Here lies poor Cora, perhaps hovering at death's door, and all you men can think to do is argue over whether the bear should have been shot or not! Really!"

Alice Banner, her brown hair tucked up under her bonnet, stood over the woman who had been knocked down, a towel and a water skin in her hands. She clucked like an irate mother hen, then knelt and applied water to the towel. "Isn't Cora's life more important than your petty disagreements?"

Nate realized he had forgotten all about Cora Webster in the flush of anger that had seized him. Annoyed at himself, he stepped toward the unconscious woman, but the rest got there first. He let them tend her, studying their faces as they did, wondering what in the world he had gotten himself into by agreeing to hire out as a guide to these three brave couples on their way to the far-off Oregon Territory.

Simon Banner was easy to read, stubborn, proud, and hotheaded. His wife, Alice, was by contrast good-natured and always considerate of others, but feisty when crossed. Next, in terms of age, came Neil and Cora Webster, both pleasant enough but quite reserved, tending to keep to themselves even during the supper hour. Harry and Eleanor Nesmith were the youngest husband and wife, and it was the impulsive Harry who was directly to blame for Cora's condition.

Nate saw someone else hasten toward the clustered group, the last member of their little party, sixteen-year-old Libbie Banner. He rarely got to see her because her father made her stay in the family's wagon practically all the time. She was a blue-eyed blonde, endowed with the kind of full figure that drew suitors like honey drew ants.

He had initially been quite flabbergasted to find her with the group since there was little in the way of a social life awaiting her in Oregon. Very few settlers had gone out there so far; the last group had consisted of Methodist missionaries the year before. To his knowledge, there wasn't anyone else her age, or even close to it, living in the Willamette Valley. In effect, by taking her with them, her parents were banishing her to a life of loneliness. Or perhaps they were counting on more settlers arriving later on. He didn't rightly know and didn't feel it was his business to pry.

Now, as Libbie joined the others, Simon looked around and saw her. "Get back to the wagon, girl," he ordered sternly.

"But Mrs. Webster—" Libbie said in her musical voice.

"She's coming around," Simon said. "Cora probably just had the wind knocked out of her." He pointed at the first wagon. "Do as I told you and get back in there."

"Yes, Pa," Libbie said, her slender shoulders slumping as she did his bidding.

Nate's forehead creased in thought but he said nothing. Were he the girl's father, he certainly wouldn't treat her in the hard fashion Simon did. It was not his place, though, to intervene. Some parents, he knew, were much stricter than others. Simon Banner could do as he pleased. But given the man's disposition, Nate figured the poor girl must be going through living hell.

Cora Webster's eyelids fluttered. She abruptly revived and sat up, screeching at the top of her lungs, "The bear! The bear!"

"It's all right, dear," Alice Banner said, taking Cora's hands in hers. "You're perfectly safe. That horrible beast is dead thanks to Mr. King."

"It is?" Cora said, gazing around in wide-eyed bewilderment. Then she spotted the body. Exhaling in relief, she sadly shook her head and said, "I tried to get out of the way, but I just couldn't. It was as if I turned to stone."

"There's no need to explain yourself," Alice soothed her. "The sight of a charging bear is enough to petrify any soul."

Until that moment Neil Webster, a skinny man sporting a walrus mustache, had stayed to one side, allowing Alice to restore his wife to her senses. Moving nearer, he bent down and took hold of Cora's arm. "Come. I'll get you into our wagon where you can rest from your ordeal."

"Perhaps she should be examined for broken bones," Alice suggested.

"I feel fine," Cora said. "Truly. There's no cause to worry yourself on my account."

"We're all in this venture together, aren't we?" Alice responded. "We must stick together through thick and thin if we hope to reach the promised land safely."

Nate walked to his stallion. The "promised land" was the phrase most often used of late to describe the verdant splendor of the Oregon Territory. He had yet to visit the region himself, but if the tales he had heard from those who had been there were any indication, then the remote Northwest qualified as Paradise on earth. He began reloading his guns, starting with the Hawken.

Simon Banner cleared his throat. "We'll stay here another hour to give Cora plenty of time to rest."

"No, we won't," Nate said as he opened his powder horn. "We're leaving just as soon as all of you get on your wagons."

"What?" Simon said, turning. "Why, pray tell?"

"Because we're still five hours shy of South Pass. We're still in Sioux country, and they can't always be counted on to be friendly. Sometimes they are. Sometimes they're out for scalps."

Banner surveyed the sea of waving grass surrounding the stand. "Did you see some Sioux while you were scouting up ahead?"

"No."

"Then we're perfectly safe, hidden among these trees."

With the patient air of a teacher instructing a six-year-old, Nate explained while he worked. "On the prairie sound travels a long ways. At night you'll hear wolves howling and swear they're right outside your camp when they're far off." He began pouring the right amount of black powder into his palm. "A gunshot too can carry for miles if the wind is right. And since few Indians have guns, whenever they hear a shot they know white men must be responsible and they go investigate."

"So you're saying some Sioux might have heard our shots and be on their way here at this very moment?"

"You catch on quick."

The others cast nervous glances in all directions, except for Alice Banner, who made straight for her wagon, saying over her shoulder, "You heard the man, husband. Let's not dally. We've put too many miles behind us to end up as fly bait."

Her words galvanized everyone into action. Harnesses were checked, water skins and whatever else they had removed from their wagons were placed back on, and the husbands assisted their wives in climbing up.

Nate tucked the reloaded flintlocks under his belt, one on either side of his large metal buckle, gripped his rifle, and swung onto the stallion. All eyes were on him, and he could well imagine the picture he must present. Dressed in fringed, beaded buckskins, with a large butcher knife on his left hip, a tomahawk on his right, and his powder horn and ammunition pouch slanted across his broad chest, he looked every inch as wild and barbaric as the Indians they dreaded. His mane of black hair spilling from under his beaver hat only added to the impression. But anyone familiar with Indians would brand him as a white man right away; there wasn't an Indian alive who had the striking green eyes he did. "Head out and keep the wagons close together," he directed.

Pleasant thoughts of his wife and son filtered through his mind as he assumed the lead. Leaving them for extended periods, such as when he went off to trap beaver, was never easy. He always feared hostile Indians would find their cabin while he was away and slay them.

In recent years the trapping trips took him farther and farther afield, compounding his worry.

The life of a free trapper had changed dramatically in recent years, and he often wished things were like they were when he first started. In 1828, when he ventured into the Rockies with his Uncle Zeke, beaver were plentiful along every mountain stream and creek. Nine years later the relentless trapping had reduced their population drastically. If a man wanted to obtain prime pelts, he had to trek into isolated areas no one else had visited. And such areas were few and far between.

Some of the old-timers, including his best friend and mentor Shakespeare McNair, believed the days of the trapping fraternity were numbered. In McNair's case it hardly mattered since Shakespeare was getting on in years and was content to quietly pass his time at home with his lovely Flathead wife.

But to Nate the decline of the beaver trade meant a world of difference. He had a family to feed, clothe, and otherwise provide for. Supplying the necessities was still relatively easy; all he had to do was bring down a deer or a buffalo and they had meat on the table and hides for making clothes. In that respect, he lived much like his Indian friends.

Nate wanted more out of life, though. He wanted to be able to give his loved ones more than the simple necessities. He also wanted to set a nest egg aside for the future, for the days when he would be too old to trap or to do much hunting— provided he lived that long. And besides all that, he needed work, needed something to do to keep himself busy.

Jim Bridger, a man Nate respected highly, claimed many more emigrants would be heading to the Oregon Territory in the years to come, and that there would be a great need for reliable guides since most settlers "couldn't find their backsides with both hands and a mirror, let alone find their way to the Pacific Coast." And Bridger, Nate believed, was right.

Which was another reason he had agreed to take the Banner party to Fort Hall. They were going to pay him one hundred dollars for his services, a sizeable sum that would tide his family over until his next prolonged trapping trip. And if he found the experience agreeable, he might set his sights on hiring out again as a guide in the future. He made a mental note to buy old Isaac Fraeb a couple of bottles of whiskey to show his gratitude for being recommended for the job.

The creak and rattle of a wagon as it drew even with the stallion brought Nate's reflection to an end and he glanced to his right.

"I wanted to have a few words with you," Simon Banner said, flicking the reins with his brawny hands. His team, four sturdy horses well accustomed to hauling freight wagons, responded superbly.

"What about?" Nate asked.

"Do you think we'll reach Fort Hall on time?"

"We should."

"I don't want to be late. The man my brother-in-law is sending to meet us and take us the rest of the way might not wait around very long if we don't show up by the first of July."

"Don't worry, Mr. Banner. I'll get you there."

"But I *do* worry, King. I have the lives of my family and these other good people to think of. In effect we've put our fate in your hands, and I, for one, am still waiting to be convinced that you are every bit the able frontiersman Isaac claimed."

"If you're not happy with me, I'll ride off now and you can go your own way," Nate said. He looked at Alice Banner, touched his hand to his hat, and went to turn his horse.

"Now hold on!" Simon blurted. "I didn't mean to insult you, and I certainly don't want you to leave us alone out here in the middle of nowhere."

"Perhaps, husband," Alice said, "it would be best if you kept as tight a rein on your tongue as you do on the team."

Nate saw Simon flush scarlet and smiled at Alice. Of them all, she was the friendliest, the one he liked the best. She reminded him of an aunt back in New York, a practical, no-nonsense sort of woman who always spoke her piece and wasn't cowed by anyone.

"What lies on the trail ahead?" Simon asked quickly to cover his embarrassment.

"Past South Pass we'll make for the Green River. From there, we head northwest until we reach the Snake River area and Fort Hall."

"You make it sound so easy."

"It's not," Nate admitted. "There will be days at a stretch when we'll need to ration our water. Grass for the horses will be hard to find at times. There will be steep grades to deal with and deep rivers to cross. And every step of the way we'll have to keep our eyes peeled for Indians out to count coup." He stared at the white canvas top covering the bed of the wagon. "I never thought to ask. You folks did bring foofaraw, didn't you?"

"Bring what?" Alice inquired.

"Sorry, ma'am. Foofaraw is trapper talk for trade things like ribbons, beads, trinkets, and whatnot."

Alice laughed lightly. "What a funny term! You mountain men sure do invent colorful words."

Nate straightened. That was the first time anyone had ever referred to *him* as a mountain man. He'd heard and used the expression before, usually in reference to old coons like Shakespeare who had lived in the rugged mountains nearly all of their eventful lives. But he had never regarded himself as being a true mountain man since he hadn't lived in the Rockies half as long as most of the few old-timers still alive. He was a free trapper, plain and simple.

"I'm afraid we didn't bring much to trade," Simon Banner was saying. "No one told us we would need to."

The statement worried Nate. He hadn't thought to check their provisions when Isaac led him to where they were camped out on the prairie three days ago, and that oversight might cause problems later on if they hadn't brought all they should. "How many guns does your party have?" he asked.

"Each man has two rifles," Simon said, "and Harry and I each brought pistols along."

"Good. There's no telling when they might come in handy."

"Perhaps sooner than you think," Alice remarked, pointing due west.

Nate shifted, and there, riding hard toward them, was a band of six warriors mounted on sleek, painted war ponies. As he laid eyes on the band, the Indians whooped and waved their weapons overhead.

Chapter Two

No two Indian tribes dressed exactly alike or wore their hair in the exact same style. Although many Plains tribes and some mountain dwellers relied extensively on the buffalo for everything from their clothing to their cooking utensils and their lodge furnishings, they displayed an endless variety in making these items that never ceased to fascinate Nate. In one tribe the men wore loose-fitting, plain shirts, while in another the men went in for elaborate beadwork, in another long fringes. In one tribe the parflaches might be small and hand-painted; in another, large and adorned with bright beads. Even the cradleboards used by mothers to carry young children were unique with each tribe.

So it was that Nate recognized the band galloping swiftly toward him as a roving war party of Sioux. He hefted the Hawken and braced for the worst. Three wagons loaded with goods might be more of a temptation than the warriors would let pass. He was about to raise his hand, to use sign language to tell the Sioux not to get too close, when they angled to the north, still whooping and waving their bows and lances. He noticed a tall warrior in the lead held a long stick from which dangled three long locks of black hair, and then he understood.

"Simon, don't!"

Nate turned to see Simon Banner taking aim with a rifle. "You heard your wife!" he snapped. "They won't bother us if we don't bother them."

"How can you be sure?" Simon responded skeptically.

"See that man in the front?"

"The buck carrying that stick?" Simon leaned forward, his eyes narrowing. "What are those things hanging from it?"

"Scalps."

"My word!" Alice exclaimed.

"They're on their way back to their village after a successful raid on one of their enemies," Nate detailed. "Right now they're just taunting us, letting us know they're great warriors and that they're not afraid of us. But they don't mean any harm. They're in a hurry to reach their people so they can show off the scalps they took and tell about the coup they counted. The tribe will throw a victory dance for them, and they'll likely celebrate for days."

"How primitive," Alice said.

Nate was about to point out that victories won in battle were big events in Indian life when he spotted Harry Nesmith, perched on the seat of the second wagon, lifting the Kentucky. "No!" he roared, and goaded the stallion into a run that brought him to the wagon in seconds. "Don't fire!" he commanded. Then he gazed at the last wagon to verify Neil Webster wasn't about to commit the same mistake. "They'll leave us alone if we don't start anything."

In confirmation, the band was soon little more than black dots racing across the limitless expanse of verdant prairie.

"From here on out," Nate said to Harry, "no one will fire a gun without first getting my say-so. And that includes you, Nesmith. You're a mite too bloodthirsty for my taste. If you're not careful, you'll get us into a heap of trouble before this trip is done."

Young Nesmith bristled. "This is my gun," he declared, holding the Kentucky out over the edge of his seat, "and I'll shoot it any damn time I please."

Nate didn't waste time in further debate. He simply reached up, grabbed the Kentucky, and pulled with all the might in his arm and shoulder before Nesmith could think to let go. Which was sufficient to yank Harry clean off of the wagon seat and to send him sailing head over heels for a good dozen feet to tumble onto the ground with a resounding thud.

Cora Nesmith screamed.

Sliding down, Nate walked up to Harry, who had both hands on the ground and was attempting to stand. Without warning, without ceremony, he slammed the stock of the Hawken into the side of Harry's head and Nesmith crumpled like an empty sack of potatoes. Angry shouts from the right and the left made him look up.

Both Simon Banner and Neil Webster were converging on the spot.

"What's the meaning of this outrage?" Banner demanded rudely. "You're supposed to guide and protect us, not attack us!"

"True enough," Nate said, "but I didn't figure on having to protect you from *yourselves*. And I'm fed up with having every word I say tossed back in my face." He glared at the two pilgrims. "From here on out, all of you will do as I say when I say it. One more argument, one more time where one of you thinks he knows better than I do how to survive out here, and you'll be on your own. Savvy?"

"You don't mean that," Neil Webster said.

"Yes, he does," Simon stated, kneeling to examine Harry. "All right, King. We'll do things your way. But I want you to know I'm not accustomed to having any man tell me how to live my life."

Nate spun on his heels and stepped to the stallion.

"You're a hard man, King," Simon added.

"The Rockies make a man that way," Nate said, mounting. "Nature has her lessons to teach, and the man who fails to learn them doesn't last long. The wilderness is no place for weaklings, cowards, or pigheaded fools." He rode up to the first wagon, then stopped and looked back to observe Nesmith being slapped to life.

"Mr. King?" Alice said softly.

"Yes, ma'am?"

"Please forgive my husband and the other men. They're really decent, hard-working men at heart, and they don't bear you any ill will." She surveyed the unknown land to the west. "It's not easy taking the biggest step of your entire life, risking everything that you own and those you love the most, and not knowing how things will turn out in the end."

"If you don't mind my saying so, ma'am, your husband will do right fine with you by his side. Every hothead needs a wise woman like yourself to show him when he's making a fool of himself."

"Mr. King! I'm blushing!"

Grinning, Nate rode slowly forward. Soon the wagons were in motion again, and the next five hours passed uneventfully. Added to the rattling of the wagons and the dull thud of weary hoofs was the rustling of the wind through the high grass. Occasionally rabbits bounded away in bursts of incredible speed. Prairie dogs whistled shrilly to warn their fellows or chattered angrily at the intruders. Deer and antelope kept respectful distances.

Once a small herd of buffalo interrupted their grazing to watch the lumbering wagons go by.

Nate liked the plains, but nowhere near as much as he liked the mountains. Give him the snow-crowned peaks, the crystal-clear high country lakes, the virgin pine forests teeming with wildlife, and he was content. On the prairie he felt too exposed, too vulnerable. There were few places for a man to seek shelter if set upon.

Consequently, he was relieved when South Pass finally rose into sight. The mountains themselves had appeared much sooner, at first as vague blue shapes shimmering on the horizon. To the north lay the Wind River Range. To the south rose the Green Mountains. Between them lay the single most accessible pass through the entire chain of foreboding Rockies, a wide, gently sloping sandy saddle that wagons could negotiate with ease.

South Pass had been used regularly by Indians for ages; by white men ever since the early 1820's, when enterprising trappers had availed themselves of the gateway to enter the previously unexplored Green River country, which turned out to be a prime trapping region. The annual caravans bearing supplies from St.Louis to the various Rendezvous sites all relied on South Pass, and only the year before the caravan had included a number of wagons.

All this Nate knew well, and it was why he had guided the emigrants straight to the pass from their camp on the Plains. He was mildly surprised to note deep ruts in the soil left by the wagons that had gone over the pass the year before, and he idly wondered how scarred the earth would be if great numbers of wagons were to head westward in the years to come as Bridger and Shakespeare contended would be the case.

He was constantly alert for Indians. Availing himself of the slope, he turned in his saddle and scanned the prairie they were leaving behind. The endless sea of grass shimmered in the sunlight, stretching to the eastern horizon, broken only by scattered stands of trees and a knoll or two. There was ample game in evidence but no sign of Indians.

It would be a minor miracle if they reached Fort Hall without running into hostiles. The Green River country they were about to cross was a favorite stamping ground of the highly feared Blackfoot confederacy, consisting of the formidable Blackfeet themselves and their two allies, the Bloods and the Piegans. Of the three the Blackfeet were by far the worst, waging war as they did not only on all whites but also on every other tribe outside the confederacy. They were the bane of the Shoshones, Crows, and Nez Percé, all friends to the whites.

Nate had tangled with the Blackfeet on more occasions than he cared to count, and had no desire to go up against them again. If he should be killed, the pilgrims wouldn't stand a prayer. The Blackfeet would show no mercy, not even to the women. In fact, the women might suffer a worse fate than the men, who would undoubtedly be tortured before being slain. Some of the Blackfeet might be inclined to take the white women into their lodges, perhaps for the novelty, in effect banishing their captives to a life of perpetual slavery, to daily backbreaking toil, and much worse, to never-ending harsh treatment at the hands of the Blackfoot women.

Suddenly Nate heard a snort, then a low grunt, both from the other side of the pass. He was almost to the top, and he hefted his Hawken as he rode high enough to see the land unfold to the west. There were mountains and valleys and canyons galore. But much closer was a sight so unexpected that he reined up in astonishment.

Hundreds and hundreds of shaggy buffaloes were coming directly toward him.

He realized a large herd was on its way onto the prairie and the wagons were right in the path of the great brutes. If a stampede started, the settlers would be caught right in the middle. There was no time to swing wide and wait for the herd to pass because the foremost bulls were less than two hundred yards away. Something else had to be done, and quickly.

Nate wheeled the stallion and raced to the first wagon. "Buffalo!" he warned them, waving for the other wagons to close the gap. "Bunch up and sit tight. If the critters stampede, get in the beds of your wagons and lie low."

Nesmith and Webster brought up their wagons rapidly and positioned themselves on either side of Banner's wagon. No sooner did they stop than the first line of lumbering bison appeared.

Buffalo were completely unpredictable. A herd might flee at the mere sight of a man, or it might stand its ground until fired upon. Once panicked, a herd was transformed into an unstoppable force of Nature, rolling over everything in its way, covering scores of miles in uncontrolled flight. Indians used this trait to their advantage by driving herds over cliffs. In one day thousands of bison might be killed, providing enough hides and meat to last many months.

Individually buffalo were equally formidable. The bulls stood six feet at the shoulder and possessed horn spreads of three feet. Weighing upwards of two thousands pounds, they could bowl over a horse and rider with ease. And the cows were not all that much smaller.

Now a surging tide of brutes eager for the lush prairie grass swept over the rim of South Pass and down the gradual slope, venting a chorus of grunts, snorts, and bellows as they advanced.

Nate had moved into the narrow space between the Banner and Webster wagons, where the stallion couldn't be inadvertently gored. He didn't know how tightly the herd would press them and feared a stampede at any second. The pale faces of the settlers showed they shared his anxiety.

The buffaloes drew steadily nearer. Nate could see their nostrils flaring as they breathed, see their hairy sides rippling as they walked. The wind bore their strong scent to him, mingled with the dust raised by thousands of pounding hoofs. Already the leading ranks had become aware of the wagons and horses in their path, and the next moment those ranks parted, some bearing to the left, others to the right, giving the wagons a wide berth.

Nate hoped none of the women would cry out. Even a frightened whinny from one of the horses could set the bison into thunderous motion. He sat perfectly still and held the stallion the same way. On the wagon seats were six statues. Every member of the party was as rigid as a rock. Except for Libbie. He saw her peek out over her mother's shoulder, agog at the number of buffalo. If she only knew. This was a big herd, but it was nowhere near the biggest Nate had seen. Once, he'd sat and watched for a whole day as an unending stream of the great beasts flowed southward.

A passing bull suddenly bellowed and gave the wagons a wary look, then lowered its head and swung its wicked horns. But the swing was more of a defensive act than an outright attack, and neither horn came into contact with Webster's wagon or the horses.

Nate spotted calves here and there and heard their distinctive bawling. Usually born in May or early June, calves were able to stand 30 minutes after their birth, to walk within an hour or two, and within two days could join the herd on its travels. At two months their horns sprouted, as did their telltale humps.

The air filled with dust. Flies buzzed by. Harry Nesmith had a coughing fit until Nate glanced sharply at him. Around the wagons arose the ceaseless sounds of the

herd. Minute after minute dragged by with awful slow-
ness. Nate felt the stallion fidget and saw the teams doing
the same. He wondered if he had miscalculated, if the herd
was much larger than he thought. Then to his delight, the
number of buffalo dwindled. Fewer and fewer went past.
At the rear of the herd walked the old ones and the sick, the
inevitable stragglers, those most likely to be picked off by
wolves out on the prairie.

"Praise the Lord that's over!" Alice exclaimed when the
last of the buffalo had gone by.

"I hope I never go through that again!" Neil Webster
said. "Did you see the way those monsters were looking
at us? I thought they'd charge us for sure."

Simon was staring at Nate. "Are there a lot of buffalo
between here and Fort Hall? Will this happen again?"

"This was a fluke," Nate said, moving in front of the
wagons. "Most herds in the mountains are small. But at
this time of the year they like to head out onto the prairie,
and that's when they form into big groups like the one
we've just seen." He motioned for the wagons to resume
rolling.

"If there *is* a next time, try to give us more warning,"
Simon commented resentfully. "We could have been
killed."

Nate controlled his temper and rode to the crest. The
ground was marred by thousands of hoofprints and drop-
pings. Putting a hand above his eyes to shield them from
the brilliant sunlight, he studied the lay of the land,
reacquainting himself with the more prominent land-
marks. He had a certain destination in mind, a valley
watered by a bubbling brook, that he wanted to reach
before dark.

The teams were exhausted by the time he called a halt,
and when the men released the horses from harness, the
animals plodded into the water and stood there drinking
greedily. He watered his stallion before getting down to

business, which entailed giving advice on how best to set up the camp.

With the sun sinking below the western horizon in a blazing display of vivid colors, a welcome cool breeze sprang up from the northwest. Soon Harry Nesmith had a crackling fire going and the women were busy preparing stew for supper. Nate had bagged a black-tailed buck the evening before, and there was enough meat left for a feast.

Nate sat on a log near the fire, a twig between his teeth, and listened to the conversations around him. As yet he was treated like an outsider and rarely invited to throw in his two cents worth unless they needed his opinion in his capacity as their guide. He didn't mind their attitude all that much. Years of living in the mountains, of being self-reliant and independent, had taught him that what others said or did could have no effect on him unless he let it. And he wasn't about to let a bunch of uppity Easterners upset him.

Alice Banner came over. "Mr.King, would you care for bread with your stew tonight? We have plenty, and I'm more than happy to share with you."

"You're a kind woman, Mrs. Banner. You remind me a lot of my wife."

"I do?" Alice said, smiling self-consciously. She was a robust woman, in her late forties or early fifties, and her hair, what little could be seen hanging from under her prim bonnet, was flecked with premature gray. "I gather you must love your wife very much."

"That I do."

"Do you find it hard . . . ?" Alice began, then caught herself. "What I mean to say is, do you like . . . ?" Again she stopped, and clasped her hands.

"Do I like being married to an Indian woman?" Nate finished for her. There was no sarcasm in her tone, no spite in her eyes, just simple curiosity, as well there might be in a woman who had lived her entire life in a sheltered farming community back in the States. "Yes, ma'am. I do. Winona is beautiful, caring, and intelligent. She speaks English better than I can speak her tongue, which says a lot because English is hard for most Indians to pick up."

"Speaking of English," Alice said, "I've noticed that you are a cut above most frontiersmen we've met. Many of them use atrocious grammar and the worst sort of profanity." She cocked her head. "You, I take it, are a literate man."

"I was born and raised in New York City," Nate said, and lowered his voice as if confiding a dark secret. "Don't let it get around, but I can read and write with the best of 'em. I'm a big admirer of James Fenimore Cooper."

"Cooper? Isn't he the one who writes those marvelous books about Indians and such? *The Last of the Mohicans* was one of his works, was it not?"

"You know your literature, ma'am."

"Not really," Alice said, and sighed. "I keep up on current events through newspapers and friends, but Simon limits our reading to the Bible. He believes that all other books are tainted by the Devil's influence."

"Even books like Cooper's? Nate asked. This was the first he had ever heard of such a notion and he didn't quite know how to take it.

"Especially those kinds of books. Simon says they offer a man's view of the world when what we really need to know is God's view." She glanced around and saw her husband moving toward the fire. "Now if you'll excuse me, I'd better finish with supper." Off she hastened.

Nate rose and stretched. He was a religious man himself, insomuch as he believed there was a God and he tried to live the Golden Rule as much as possible given the harsh nature of life in the wilderness, but the idea of being allowed to read from only the Bible struck him as fanatical. What about all the other great thoughts and beautiful sentiments that had been expressed by writers down through the ages? Didn't they count for anything?

He shook his head, grabbed the Hawken, and began to make a circuit of the camp. Stars had blossomed in the heavens. There were trees close at hand, aspens and others, and their leaves rustled in the wind. Cradling the rifle, he made sure the horses were all tethered, then turned.

From in the trees came a soft noise.

Nate was in a crouch in a flash, the Hawken leveled and cocked. A quick look at the fire revealed all three couples were accounted for. The noise was repeated over and over. It sounded like a low moan, as if someone was in pain. Puzzled, he worked his way into the trees and halted. Now it sounded like someone crying.

On cat's feet he stalked forward until he saw a familiar figure leaning on a trunk and sobbing uncontrollably. He rose and took a step backward, not wanting to intrude on her privacy, but his heel crunched down on a dry twig that snapped loudly and she whirled like a cornered animal, fear lining her features until she saw him.

"Mr. King!"

"Sorry, Libbie," Nate said. Something inside told him to keep his voice low so her parents wouldn't overhear. "I didn't mean to bother you. I'm leaving."

"I just needed some air," Libbie said, swiping at her damp eyes. She sniffled and gazed over his shoulder. "Is my pa hunting for me?"

"No."

Libbie nodded and dabbed at her eyes with her right sleeve. "I guess I'm more miserable over leaving all my friends and kin than I thought."

"I know how rough it can be," Nate said.

"Do you?" Libbie responded. She squared her shoulders and walked forward. "Life is rougher on some of us than on others."

"Strange words coming from one so young."

That stopped her. "Do you have to be an adult to know a broken heart? To have all your hopes and dreams ruined? To have the only true happiness you've ever known torn from you?"

"I reckon not."

Then she was gone, darting through the trees and to the wagons, coming on them from the rear so no one at the fire would notice. She vanished inside her parents' wagon in a swirl of blond hair.

What the dickens was that all about? Nate asked himself, moving into the open. He's seen her face as she went by, a face mirroring uncommon inner torment for a sixteen-year-old. True, by frontier standards a sixteen-year-old was considered a grown-up. But Libbie was from back East, and her parents were the sort to zealously safeguard their daughter from anything that might harm her. Hard as nails Simon Banner might be, yet there was no denying the man cared for his family.

Nate scanned the encampment, gazed to the south, to the north, and the east. And froze, a tingle of apprehension rippling down his spine. For in the distance, at about where South Pass should be, was a yellow pinpoint of light that could only be one thing.

It was another campfire.

Chapter Three

At night, when the pristine landscape was plunged in shrouding darkness, flickering campfires stood out like lighthouse beacons sweeping the sea, a certain lure for possible enemies. Which was why experienced frontiersmen and Indians alike took particular pains to build their fires where the flames couldn't be seen from any great distance. Only a fool who wanted to die advertised his presence in the wilderness.

Nate had picked their campsite wisely in that respect. The narrow valley in which he had called a halt opened to the east, and there were trees at the valley mouth that served as an effective screen from possible prying eyes. He always had the safety of the Banner party uppermost in mind when he selected places to stop.

But whoever had set up camp near the top of South Pass, he reflected, was just asking for trouble. The fire was high up where it could be seen for miles around. Since no Indian in his right mind would ever be so foolish, the fire must have been built by white men. Greenhorns, at that.

Nate walked to the fire, where the women were busy preparing the meal and the men were huddled together in conversation. "We're not alone," he informed them.

All six of them stopped whatever they were doing to look at him.

"What's that?" Simon asked.

"We have neighbors," Nate said, raising his right arm and pointing. Eleanor Nesmith gasped. One of the men muttered an oath.

"Indians, you think?" Neil Webster inquired anxiously.

"Not likely," Nate said. "But we'll know soon enough. I figure to ride back there and see who it is."

Simon turned. *"Now?"*

"I don't like the fact that they're right on our trail. It could be a coincidence. Then again, it might not. This is the perfect time to find out. I can get close to their camp without them noticing, and if they strike me as being unfriendly, I'll persuade them to stop following us."

"But if they're white men they must be friendly," Alice said.

"Not necessarily, ma'am. There are some nasty sorts out here who are worse than hostile Indians. Some years ago I had a run-in with a wicked bunch who went around killing trappers for their money. Another time I tangled with some white men who kidnapped my wife. And I shouldn't forget Crazy George, who took a fancy to human flesh and ate other folks."

The women were aghast.

"This Crazy George was a cannibal?" Cora Webster said, a dainty hand pressed to her pale throat.

"That he was," Nate confirmed. "He confessed to eating about eight people before he met his Maker. It seems he got started one winter when he was snowed in way up in the Rockies. He ran out of food, couldn't hunt game, and decided the only way he would survive until spring was if he ate the Indian woman who lived with him."

Cora appeared about to faint. "How disgusting," she said weakly.

"The man was clearly not in his right mind," Elizabeth Nesmith declared. She moved closer to her husband and he draped a protective arm around her shoulder.

"Why tell us this and scare the women so?" Harry Nesmith asked, his resentment transparent. "First you take me by surprise and almost cave in my skull, and now you're deliberately frightening the women. If you ask me, you're a poor excuse for a guide."

"I didn't ask you," Nate shot back. "And if I'd been trying to bust your head open instead of teaching you a lesson, you'd be feeding the worms right this minute." He nodded at the distant firelight. "I didn't tell you about my experiences just to scare you, but to let you know that some white men are as evil as can be so you'll be on your guard until you get to your destination."

"How nice of you," Simon said dryly. "But I'm more concerned about having you up and leave us at a time like this. What if something happens to you? How will we reach Fort Hall?"

"It's a two hour ride to the pass if I push my horse," Nate answered. "With luck I'll be back before midnight."

"I don't want you to go," Simon stubbornly persisted.

"Would you rather be taken by surprise by a pack of cutthroats out to steal everything you own?" Nate snapped, and when no one made a reply he pivoted and retrieved his saddle and Epishemore. His was typical of the square pieces of buffalo robes used by the trapping fraternity under their saddles to keep their mounts from being chafed. He walked to the stallion, and with a deft flip aligned the Epishemore on its back. Then he applied the saddle.

The settlers had followed him.

"At least take one of us with you," Simon proposed. "You might need help."

"I can manage quite well on my own," Nate said. "You'll be busy keeping watch here. Until I return, have a man on guard at all times. And remember to snuff out the fire after you're done with your meal."

"Be careful, King."

Nate glanced at him. Was Banner genuinely concerned about his welfare or only thinking of how hard it would be for the emigrants to survive on their own? He gave the man the benefit of the doubt. "Thanks. I always am." The Hawken clutched in his left hand, he swung up. "By midnight," he said, and rode eastward.

Despite the long hours of travel put in earlier, the stallion was rested and raring to go. "Come on, Pegasus," he said softly, using the name he had given the horse when it was presented to him by the Nez Percé. He gave the animal an affectionate pat on the neck. "Let's get this over with so I can get some sleep tonight."

He gave the stallion its head, feeling the cool air caress his face and fan his hair. His stomach rumbled, reminding him he should have snatched a bite to eat before leaving. Off to the right an owl hooted. To the left, deep in the forest, a wolf howled and was immediately answered by another.

Without the overloaded wagons to slow him down, he reached South Pass in half the time it otherwise would have taken. Had it been daylight he would have gotten there even sooner. But at night a rider had to be extra careful to avoid obstacles and holes that might harm his mount. So he held the stallion to a trot instead of going at a gallop.

The pungent odor of wood smoke tingled his nose as he entered pines to the south of the pass and slowly worked his way closer to the campfire. He tied Pegasus two hundred yards from his goal to prevent any horses in the camp from detecting the stallion's scent and acting up, thus alerting whoever was there.

Nate loosened both flintlocks under his belt, then crouched and stalked upward until he could see a pair of clean-shaven men seated in front of the dancing flames. Both were white, both wearing homespun clothes. Working his way to the last of the trees, he flattened and crawled to within 15 feet of the unsuspecting pair. They were eating heartily, chomping and slurping soup from tins. Four horses were tethered across the way.

"Tomorrow, you reckon?" the heftier of the duo suddenly asked.

"I don't rightly know," responded his lean companion.

"You'd better make up your mind soon."

"I will. But we don't want to rush things."

"You're not turning yellow, are you? Not after all he put you through?"

"No. Of course not."

"Then I say we do it tomorrow."

"We bide our time and wait for the right chance."

The hefty one shifted to stare at the lean one. "Damn it all, Brian! I knew you'd do this! I knew you'd drag my ass into this godforsaken wilderness and then get cold feet. If you were a real man you would have done what needs to be done long ago."

"Shut up and finish eating."

Nate guessed that neither man was much over 20 years old, if that, and as green as they came. They wouldn't live to get much older either at the rate they were going. He inched his way around until he was behind them, then rose slowly, the Hawken in both hands. The hammer made a loud click when he thumbed it back. "Not a move, gentlemen, unless you want some lead in your diet."

The hefty one started and dropped his soup, the tin clanging against a small rock bordering the fire. His companion, the man named Brian, stiffened with a sharp intake of breath. Neither made a play for their rifles, which were lying in plain sight beside them.

"So far, so good," Nate said, stepping closer. He slanted to the left until he could see their faces, and grinned when they gaped in surprise.

"Are you an Injun?" the hefty one blurted out.

"No, but thanks for the compliment," Nate responded. He wagged the Hawken. "You can keep eating if you want, but don't try to touch your rifles or you'll spring a leak."

"Who are you? What do you want?" Brian asked. He was a handsome youth with black hair and blue eyes. His skin was tanned, his chin cleft. A two-inch scar on his right cheek ran from below his right eye to the corner of his mouth.

"The handle is Nate King. Some hereabouts call me Grizzly Killer."

The hefty one gulped. "What kind of a name is that?"

"It's my Indian name, given to me by a Cheyenne warrior after I killed my first grizzly," Nate disclosed, stepping to within a yard of Brian and hunkering down, the Hawken leveled and steady. "The name stuck. Now the Cheyennes, the Shoshones, the Flatheads, they all call me Grizzly Killer." He paused. "Who might you two be?"

"I'm—" the hefty one began, but was promptly cut off by Brian.

"Don't say a word! We don't have to tell this guy who we are if we don't want to."

Nate leaned back. "You're not being very neighborly, young man."

Brian gave a bitter laugh. "You're a fine one to talk, mister, the way you sneak into our camp and hold us at gunpoint."

He jabbed a thumb at Nate. "And who are you calling young? Even with that beard of yours, you don't appear to me to be much over twenty-five, if that."

"All right. If you don't want to cooperate, I won't force you. But we have to palaver a bit before I cut out."

"Palaver?" the hefty one repeated.

"We need to have a talk," Nate translated, making a mental note to refrain from speaking mountain-man lingo when in the company of greenhorns. His whole vocabulary had changed remarkably since he departed New York City, and he now unconsciously spoke "mountainee jargon," as a trader at a Rendezvous had once referred to the trapper way of talking, as a matter of course. It was interesting, he mused, how a person adapted to new ways so completely that those who knew him in former times wouldn't recognize him if they saw him again.

"Talk about what?" Brian demanded.

"You two," Nate said. "Why are you trying to get yourselves killed?"

"You're crazy," the hefty one said.

"No, *you* are for building your fire near the top of South Pass, right out in the open where every Blackfoot within ten miles can see it. Or do you want a war party to pay you a visit come daylight?"

Brian glanced at the crackling flames, then out over the surrounding countryside. "We liked the view," he said softly.

"So do I, but it's not worth dying over," Nate said. "If you're smart, once I'm gone you'll move your camp down into the trees. And from now on don't camp out in the open like this."

He studied them for a minute. "I don't know what you two are doing here and it's not my rightful place to meddle. But unless you have a damn good reason, you should head for Fort Leavenworth or Independence or some other settlement just as fast as your horses will take you. Unless, of course, you're going to the Oregon Territory."

"Only part of the way—" the hefty one said, but his friend slapped his arm.

"Damn it, Pudge! Keep your mouth closed!" Brian snapped. "We don't know anything about this man. How do we know we can trust him?"

Nate was becoming annoyed. "I don't care if you trust me or not. I'm just trying to help you live a little longer." He lowered the rifle and crossed his legs. Since they wouldn't confide in him, maybe he could convince them to ride with the Banner party. He suspected there was some link between them and the settlers anyway, and this way he'd be able to keep an eye on them at all times and perhaps learn what they were up to. "At first I figured you might be cutthroats out to steal from a party I'm guiding to Fort Hall, but now I doubt whether the two of you could steal candy from a baby."

Brian's lips became thin lines.

"Face facts. Neither of you know much about the wilderness. You won't last a week in these mountains on your own. So here's an idea for you to consider. Why not join up with the group I'm guiding? There's safety in numbers, and you'd be treated to some fine home cooking every night."

"No," Brian said.

"Why not?"

"No."

"Some extra company on the trail is always welcome. What if one of you has an accident?"

"No."

"Brian, please," the one nicknamed Pudge said. "He has a good point. I would feel safer with them."

"Do you really think *he'd* let us ride along?" Brian countered.

"Who?" Nate asked.

"No one," Brian said sullenly.

"What's your connection to this group I'm with?" Nate probed. "Why are you following them?"

"None of your damn business. Now go away and leave us alone."

Nate recognized a hopeless cause when he confronted one. Pushing to his feet, he cradled the Hawken and thoughtfully regarded the pair. He doubted whether either of them posed a threat to anyone under his care, but he wasn't about to take unnecessary chances. "Since you won't be neighborly, I'm going to lay down the law. I don't want to catch either of you skulking about the people I'm with or I'm liable to shoot first and ask what you were doing later. If you want to pay us a visit, ride right up in the open where I can see you."

"You have no right ordering us around," Brian said.

"I reckon I am rubbing folks the wrong way lately, but it can't be helped. I have seven lives to think of." Nate nodded at each of them and walked off. "Don't forget about moving your camp," he said over his shoulder.

Neither of them uttered a word. Brian glared angrily, his fists clenched. Pudge appeared extremely upset, and if his expression was any indication he didn't want Nate to go.

Once Nate was back in the saddle, he glanced at the pair and saw them energetically preparing to relocate. A jab of his heels started the stallion westward. He pondered the incident as he rode, trying to make sense out of what they had said. There was little to go on. Apparently, though, Brian had a grievance against one of the emigrants. It would have been easy to force the young man to talk, but Nate balked at resorting to violence unless there was a clear and present danger to those under his care.

His best hope lay in mentioning the names of the pair to the pilgrims. The one who knew them might then provide whatever background there was to the affair. Resting the Hawken across his saddle, he rode at a leisurely pace until he came within a mile of the valley. It was then he saw the grizzly.

An immense black shape materialized to the southeast, moving northward. Nate reined up, his scalp prickling, and recognized the bear by its enormous outline and its distinctive shuffling gait. The monster was 70 feet away, at the very limit of his vision in the moonless gloom. Since the wind was blowing from the grizzly to him, it had not yet registered his scent. But the beast must have heard the stallion, so it might charge at an instant's notice.

He fingered the rifle, his eyes glued to the hulking form. Grizzlies were even more unpredictable than buffalo. Primarily nocturnal, they would attack anything that moved if they were hungry enough. And they were exceedingly hard to kill. He'd heard of a case where a grizzly had been shot 12 times, including balls in the head and lungs, yet still it kept coming.

Perhaps because he had ranged so far and wide over the plains and the mountains, it had been his misfortune to run up against more grizzlies than most mountaineers. So far he had always prevailed, but each time he'd barely escaped with his life. Trappers and Indians alike gave grizzlies wide berths, with ample cause.

Measuring over eight feet in length and standing four and a half feet high at the shoulders, grizzlies often weighed upwards of 1500 pounds. They were veritable behemoths, capable of slashing a man to ribbons with a single swipe of one of their huge forepaws. The mighty bears were, in every respect, the lords of their vast domain.

Nate's mouth went dry, his palms became damp, as he watched the bear pass in front of him and continue on. Thankfully, Pegasus stood stock still, not so much as a nostril flaring. The stallion instinctively sensed they were in great danger. Since grizzlies were capable of loping as fast as a horse over short distances, there was no guarantee Pegasus's speed would enable them to escape.

Nate heard the bear grunt a few times. Its ponderous head was close to the ground, perhaps following a scent. When the gigantic shape finally disappeared in the murk, he waited a full minute before goading the stallion forward. A quarter of a mile was covered at a gallop, then he slowed and looked back. There was no trace of pursuit. Nor did he see the campfire on South Pass. Brian and Pudge had done as he'd bid them.

Relaxing, smiling, Nate rode into the valley, passing through the trees and out into the open. The white canvas covering the wagons was a stark contrast to the inky night, and he made a beeline toward them.

Two hundred yards from the camp, Pegasus suddenly halted and gazed to the northwest. Mystified, Nate looked but saw nothing out of the ordinary. He lifted the reins, and was set to lash the stallion when he heard a low whinny. Squinting, he made out the forms of a number of horses heading northwest, and he immediately assumed some of the animals belonging to the pilgrims had strayed off.

Thinking he should catch them before they went too far, Nate angled to intercept the half dozen or so he could see. But he went just a few yards when he spied several figures walking with the horses. Puzzled, he stopped, wondering where Banner and the others could be taking the stock at that time of night. The answer, courtesy of a whispered string of words wafted on the wind, filled him with consternation.

One of those men had spoken in an Indian tongue!

The language was unfamiliar, so the Indians weren't Shoshones, Crows, Nez Perce, Flatheads, or Cheyennes. They might well be Blackfeet, in which case the odds of any of the settlers being alive were slim. But if there had been a fight, why hadn't he heard gunshots? Or had the raiders taken the whites completely by surprise and slit the

throats of all the men before a single rifle could be brought
to bear?

Nate hesitated, tempted to go after the stock but worried
about the pilgrims. Dismounting, he took the reins in his
left hand and hurried toward the freight wagons. The fire
had long since gone out. Now only the embers glowed dully. He halted 20 feet out to study the situation.

From inside the lead wagon rumbled the sound of
someone sawing logs. So at least one of them was still
breathing. Nate let the reins dangle and padded closer.
The wagons were all intact and there were no bodies
lying scattered about. He was almost to the Banner
wagon when he spotted what appeared to be a slender
log to one side. But he knew better. In two strides he
was kneeling beside the limp body of Harry Nesmith.
A hand to the man's throat revealed a slight pulse, and
a swift examination showed a nasty bump and a small
amount of warm blood on the back of Nesmith's head.
One of the Indians must have snuck up on Nesmith and
used a war club or a tomahawk to knock him out.

Nate swiveled, debating whether to awaken the rest of
the emigrants or to go after the stolen horses. The Indians
were still close enough to hear the commotion the pilgrims
were bound to make if he roused them, and he doubted
whether any of the party would be much help in a running
battle. It would be wiser, then, to try and recover the stock
alone before the Indians got much farther away.

He rose and stepped to Pegasus. Scores of yards off,
nearly to the forest, were the thieves and the horses.
Swinging up, he bent down to gather the reins in his hand.
Unexpectedly, the stallion shied.

Onrushing footsteps pounded on the earth.

Nate swept upright, twisting in the direction of
the noise, toward the wagons, and he was just in
time to see a lone warrior hurtle at him from out
of the darkness. His thumb was curling around the

hammer when the warrior leaped with arms out-spread, and before he could fire the Indian slammed into him.

They both went down.

Chapter Four

The impact of the warrior's heavy body knocked the Hawken from Nate's fingers. He fell backwards, the Indian on top, a hand clawing at his throat. The dull glint of steel told him what the warrior's other hand was doing, and he barely got his arm up in time to deflect a vicious swipe that would have sliced his throat wide open.

Nate hit hard on his shoulders and rolled, heaving the warrior from him as he did. In a twinkling he was in a crouch and drawing his butcher knife. The Indian lunged and swung but Nate skipped aside and countered. He missed. They silently circled one another. The warrior feinted but Nate didn't take the bait.

Uppermost in Nate's mind was concern that another brave would come at him from behind while he was preoccupied with the man in front of him. It was hard to tell, but he believed the warrior was a Blood or a Piegan, the two tribes allied with the Blackfeet. All three were devoted to the extermination of all whites, so using sign language to try and convince his attacker that he was friendly would be a waste of time and would only get him killed.

The warrior closed and swung again. Nate darted to the right. He felt the man's knife nick his buckskins, and he thrust out, his blade biting into the warrior's side but not going deep. The Indian promptly moved back and hissed like an enraged rattler.

Nate knew the warrior was deliberately holding him at bay long enough for the other Indians to reach cover with the stolen horses. But he must get after them before they got to the trees. Since stealth and silence no longer mattered, he streaked his left hand to the left flintlock. His fingers were wrapping around the pistol when a shrill scream pierced the night.

The Indian involuntarily glanced at the wagons.

In that instant Nate pointed the flintlock and fired, the heavy-caliber gun booming and bucking. Hit squarely in the chest, the warrior was flung onto the ground. Nate didn't linger to confirm the kill. He dashed to Pegasus, wedging the pistol under his belt as he ran, and bellowed, "Indians! They're stealing the stock! Get up and grab your guns!"

The Hawken was lying at the stallion's feet. In a twinkling Nate scooped the rifle up. He swung into the saddle, turned Pegasus to the northwest, and galloped toward the trees. The horses were still in sight, but it was doubtful he could get there before the woods closed around them. Two Indians, one on either side of the stolen animals, were urging the horses on, yipping and yelling now that they knew they had been discovered.

Nate took a chance. He tucked the Hawken to his shoulder and sighted on the center of the Indian on the right. It was the best he could do given the range and the gloom, and he mentally crossed his fingers when he squeezed the trigger. For a second the cloud of gunsmoke obscured the target; then Pegasus swept him onward and he saw the Indian prone on the ground.

The other warrior, the only one to be seen, had broken and was in full flight for the forest.

Without anyone to prod them on, the stolen horses came to a stop. Nate reloaded the Hawken, spilling some of the black powder before he poured enough down the barrel, and had the rifle cocked when he rode up to the one he had shot. A dark stain on the man's chest showed him where the ball had struck. The Indian's eyes were locked wide in death.

Circling around in front of the horses, Nate hunched low over his stallion's neck in case the lone survivor entertained the notion of taking revenge. Nothing moved in the forest. Speaking softly, he got the stock turned around and headed back toward the wagons, where a lantern had been lit and the emigrants were talking in loud, excited tones.

A few things were cleared up to his satisfaction. Now he knew why the Indians had not bothered to go after the sleeping pilgrims in the wagons. There had only been three warriors. Rather than risk someone sounding the alarm and having to face possibly superior numbers and the accurate guns of the white man, the three Indians had concentrated on getting away scot-free with the horses. One of them must have spotted him approaching and snuck up on him.

But not all his questions were answered. Why had there only been three hostiles? The only logical reason upset him tremendously for it meant the Banner party was now in dire peril. But it could have been worse. If he had not returned when he did, the whole bunch would now be stranded and without any hope of getting away.

"Look!" someone shouted. It sounded like Neil Webster.

"It's Mr. King!" This from Alice Banner.

Nate rode up and dismounted. Half of them were clustered around Harry Nesmith, the rest around the slain warrior. "Neil, I want you to take these horses and tie them good and proper to the wagons. We can't afford to lose a single one."

Webster opened his mouth as if to object, then thought better of the idea. "Whatever you say."

Simon Banner, who was on one knee beside the dead Indian and had a lantern upraised in his right hand, looked up. "Is this heathen a Blackfoot?"

"No," Nate said, going over to examine the body. The long hair parted in the middle and swept back at the front, the fringed buckskin shirt painted with symbols, and the style of moccasins confirmed his earlier hunch. "He was a Piegan."

"A what?"

"The Piegans and another tribe called the Bloods are close friends of the Blackfeet. Between them they pretty much control all the land between the upper Missouri and Saskatchewan Rivers."

Simon sighed in relief. "Thank goodness it wasn't the Blackfeet who hit us. None of us would be alive."

"You don't seem to understand," Nate said. "The Piegans and the Bloods are every bit as fierce as the Blackfeet. We're in for the fight of our lives after the one that got away tells the rest and they come after us."

Banner stood. "The rest?"

"We're nowhere near Piegan territory, which means there must be a war party in the area. These three were part of it. They were probably out scouting around when they saw our camp and they couldn't resist trying to steal our horses."

"How large do you think the war party is?"

"I've never known one to have less than ten warriors," Nate replied, gazing at Harry Nesmith. Eleanor, Harry's wife, was applying a damp cloth to his head and he was slowly reviving. The man was either incredibly lucky or had a skull as hard as granite. "Most have more. The biggest Blackfoot war party I ever heard tell of had sixty-nine."

Alice Banner, standing beside her husband, swallowed and fearfully stared at the woodland to the north. "Dear Lord! If there's that many we'll all be killed!"

"Not if I can help it," Nate assured her. He stepped nearer to Eleanor. "How is Harry?"

"He'll live, thank God," she answered, never taking her eyes off her husband. "The dirty cowards hit him from behind! They're worse than animals."

"They do what they have to," Nate said. He saw Libbie next to the wagons, a red shawl draped over her slim shoulders, her features downcast, and went over to offer an encouraging smile. "Are you all right?"

"Just dandy, Mr. King. I heard what you told my pa. How soon before the savages get here?"

"It all depends on how far their camp is from ours. I figure they'll come after us at first light, so they could show up at any time after that."

"Good."

Nate, surprised by the vehement bitterness in her voice, gazed into her eyes. What he saw there shocked him. "How can you be glad? If we get away with our scalps intact it will be a miracle."

Libbie stared at her parents, then said in a strained whisper, "I don't care. I don't care about anything anymore. If I die, so much the better."

"You're talking nonsense."

"Am I?" she retorted. "If you only knew! I deserve to die, Mr. King. It doesn't much matter to me whether I die at the hands of murderous Indians or of a broken heart. But one way or the other, I promise you I won't reach the Oregon Territory alive." With that she spun and climbed up into the Banner wagon.

Nate didn't know what to make of her attitude. Her sincerity was indisputable. But what could have so drastically soured such a young, lovely woman, on life in general and her future in particular? Something awful must have occurred, but for the life of him he couldn't think of what it might be.

"King?"

"Yes?" Nate replied absently, facing Simon, Alice, Neil, and Cora. The Nesmiths were huddled together on the ground.

"I told the others what you said about the war party," Simon declared. "We're all agreed that we should turn around and head back for St. Louis."

"And what about Oregon? What about those who are waiting for you out there?"

"Our lives are more important than reaching the promised land on time. If we head out at dawn, we should be able to reach the prairie well before the heathens show up. And on the prairie we can make better time than here in the mountains. We might be able to outrun the Piegans."

Neil Webster nodded in agreement. "At the very least we'll be able to see them coming. We'll have a better chance of defending ourselves."

"You're wrong on all counts," Nate said flatly. "In the first place, there is no way three heavy wagons can outrun the Piegans. Like the Blackfeet and the Bloods they usually conduct their raids afoot, but they can run all day if they have to and cover three times the territory a white man could in the same amount of time. If they want our hides they'll come after us no matter which way we go."

"Do you have any other objections?" Simon asked testily.

"You bet I do. In the second place, you'd be no safer out on the prairie than you are in the mountains. Piegans can sneak up through tall grass as easily as they can through pine trees, and they'd have your throats slit before you knew they were there."

"Do you have a better idea?" Neal inquired.

"Running scared isn't the answer," Nate told them. "To lick the Piegans, all we have to do is be craftier than they are. We have to outguess them every step of the way."

Alice Banner spoke up. "Do you really believe we can?"

"We have a fair chance," Nate said. "There's one thing you folks have to remember. In some respects Indians regard life as more precious than whites do. They grieve terribly whenever someone dies. Those who lose loved ones may be in mourning for months. Sometimes they chop off a finger or cut off their hair or do something else to themselves to show how much they loved the one who died."

"How barbaric!" Neil interrupted.

Nate ignored him. "They especially don't like to lose a man on a raid. It's bad medicine, the very worst kind of omen, if a war party returns bearing the news that some of the warriors died. The whole village goes into mourning."

"So what are you telling us?" Simon asked impatiently.

"That if we hold fast, if we put up a good fight and maybe kill two or three more of them, they might decide we're bad medicine and leave us alone."

Neil glanced at the dead Piegan. "But they've already lost men. Why would they bother us again?"

"They'll want revenge. And too, if they can take our scalps, if they can go back to their village with a lot of plunder, the loss of a few warriors will be easier to bear. Their people won't view the raid as a total failure." He peered up at the sparkling stars, noting the position of the Big Dipper. By his reckoning there were no more than five hours left until daylight. "If we can convince them that we'll sell our lives dearly and every scalp they try to take will cost them a man or two, they'll change their minds, turn tail, and leave."

"If we agree to go along with you, what do you want us to do?" Simon asked.

"Get set to head out right away."

"You want us to travel at night? Isn't that dangerous?"

"Not if we stick to open ground. I know this neck of the woods well, and I shouldn't have any problem finding a spot where we can make a stand. The important thing is to put a few miles behind us, to buy us some time."

"We'll talk it over," Simon said, and motioned for the others to join him as he moved to one side.

They were like frightened children, Nate reflected, ready to give up at the first grave hardship they ran into. If they were an accurate measure of the hordes of emigrants expected to one day flock to Oregon, then those untold thousands would fare better staying in the States. The frontier was no place for greenhorns, for those lacking courage. They had no idea of what they were getting themselves into. The wilderness was a harsh mistress, demanding the utmost from those who would dwell in her domain, and those who failed to take her seriously paid for their neglect with their lives. For the wild beasts and mankind alike, the unwritten law of the land was brutally simple: the survival of the fittest.

He walked to Pegasus, and happened to notice that Neil Webster had failed to tie up all the horses as he had directed. Maybe Nate was wasting his time trying to save these people. He certainly wasn't appreciated. Men like Simon and Neil thought they knew it all, thought they could do anything and everything without help from anyone else. And they resented being told what to do by someone who knew the realities of life in the wild better than they did.

Nate scratched his chin and stroked the stallion's neck. Perhaps this guiding business wasn't all it had promised to be. Was it worth the price of daily headaches over petty concerns, of having to put up with arrogant greenhorns looking down their noses at him, just so he could earn a few dollars? There were more important things in life than money. A man had his integrity to think of.

He saw Libbie peeking from the wagon and speculated on what could be bothering her. If she was so intent on dying, she might do something to give death a hand. It would be smart to keep an eye on her when possible so he could try and stop her from doing anything foolish. As if he didn't have enough to worry about.

After a minute Simon and the rest came back. The Nesmiths were now with them. Harry was pale and squinted in the bright lantern light.

"We've made up our minds," Simon announced. "We took a vote, and against my better judgment everyone has agreed to follow your lead. Our lives are in your hands."

"They have been ever since I took over from Fraeb," Nate reminded them. It was Isaac Fraeb who had initially agreed to take the emigrants from St. Louis to Fort Hall. And if Fraeb hadn't come down with a stomach sickness out on the Plains, Nate would be in his warm, cozy cabin with his wife and son right that minute. But Fraeb had become too sick to go on much farther despite trying every remedy known to whites and Indians alike. Isaac needed lots of bed rest, which he wouldn't get while acting as nursemaid for the pilgrims. So, gritting his teeth against the pain, Fraeb had ridden to ask the help of the one man he felt could handle the chore, namely Nate. And now Nate almost wished he had declined the offer.

"Do you want us to hook up the teams?" Neil inquired.

"Yes," Nate said. "We're pulling out in ten minutes." He looked at Nesmith. "Are you up to driving a wagon?"

"I'm a bit woozy," Harry said, gingerly touching his head. "And I have dizzy spells that come and go." He put a hand on his wife's shoulder. "But don't worry. Eleanor can handle a wagon as good as I can. We'll keep up with the rest."

"I hope so, for your sakes," Nate said.

The camp transformed into a whirlwind of activity as the men hastened to hook up their horses and the women filled all the water skins. Little was said. They all knew their lives were at risk, that every moment counted.

Nate took the lead, riding close to the Banner wagon. The settlers strung out in single file, a mere ten feet between the rear of each wagon and the lead horses of the next team. He took them out of the valley, then swung to the north, sticking to the open areas where the wagons made better time. They hugged the base of the mountains ringing the great basin they were in, and never strayed far from tracts of forest that would serve as their refuge should the Piegans appear sooner than Nate expected.

Traveling at night was a unique experience. The heavens were spectacular, as if a beautiful tapestry of radiant gems had been woven by divine fingers exclusively for human enjoyment. The sight was enough to take a man's breath away. And the cool breeze was a welcome contrast to the high heat of the day.

Some of the horses balked, being weary from their toils earlier, but a few cracks of a whip convinced them to forge onward. Occasionally wolves howled in the distance, or coyotes voiced their high-pitched yips. Owls, those nocturnal predators more rapacious than eagles, hooted frequently. Twice panthers vented rumbling snarls from near at hand. Every so often a rodent or some other animal would screech as it was caught in the grip of a stealthy prowler. And once, as the wagons passed a ravine, from within arose the unforgettable tremendous roaring of a grizzly. A few of the horses shied and the drivers had to calm them down before the wagons could proceed.

None of the night sounds were new to Nate. He lived with them every night, and knew them all. But he could tell the emigrants were a bit unnerved. Small wonder. It invariably surprised those who lived sheltered lives back in the States, those who conducted all their affairs while the sun was up and retired to their comfortable homes after dark, who lived in regions depleted of game, to learn that the wilderness was completely different. More animals were abroad at night than during the day, and many of them were meat-eaters that ventured out only under the cover of darkness to satisfy their cravings for raw flesh. That was why so few people ever saw panthers, bobcats, lynxes, wolverines, and the like; the animals roamed the land while the people were tucked safely in bed.

Nate held the Hawken handy, the stock resting on his right thigh, his thumb on the hammer, his finger on the trigger. It was rare for any of the big carnivores, other than grizzlies, to attack humans unless they were provoked, but he was taking no chances.

The bloodcurdling screams of the panthers underscored his hunger. Like most mountain men, he rated panther meat as downright delicious. Given a choice between a buffalo steak and a good cut of panther, ten times out of ten the mountaineers would pick the panther. Since he had not had a bite to eat since morning, he would have settled for any hot meal. Instead, he took out several pieces of jerked venison and munched on them.

Toward morning the wind picked up until it was near hurricane force, buffeting the wagons and violently shaking the canvas covers. The men had to wedge their hats down on their heads or lose them, and the women all securely tied their bonnets. Such high winds were common in the region, more so in early spring when warmer weather began to drive out the colder air.

Nate was constantly on the lookout for a suitable place to make their stand. There were plenty of gullies and ravines, but being caught in them would be a certain death warrant. He preferred high ground, somewhere with water and cover. While there were any number of hills and mountains slopes to pick from, none were ideal. There was either no water nearby or they lacked enough cover to suit him. He began to think he was being too fussy, and when the first streaks of pink and orange painted the eastern sky he resolved to find a spot soon no matter what.

Apparently Simon Banner was equally eager to stop, for he called out, "How much farther, King?"

"We'll call a halt before too long," Nate replied.

"I hope so. Our animals are on the verge of exhaustion. If the Piegans do show, we'll be stuck wherever they find us."

Shortly thereafter a ridge on the right drew Nate's attention. A gentle slope to the top was dotted with widely spaced trees, but the pines ended dozens of yards below the rim. Of more interest was what appeared to be a ribbon of water flowing down the west side. "Hold up!" he shouted, lifting his left hand. "I'll be back in a bit."

Pegasus galloped to the ridge and took the slope on the fly. Nate leaned forward to make the going easier for the stallion as its huge hoofs sent clumps of dirt flying to their rear. He made straight for the water and was overjoyed to find a small spring sheltered by boulders just below the crest. From the top he could see for miles in all directions. The opposite slope was charred black, the consequence of a fire triggered by a lightning strike on a gigantic tree that still stood, although the trunk was split down the middle and most of the limbs had been blasted off. With the vegetation burned away, there were few hiding places on the far slope the hostiles could take advantage of.

"This will have to do," Nate said, moving along the rim. The top consisted of an acre of flat ground, more than ample space for parking the wagons. Nodding in satisfaction, he moved to the west side and rose in the saddle to beckon the emigrants to join him. But as he raised his arm, he paused.

To the south, advancing at a determined dogtrot, was a long line of figures.

They were too far off for Nate to note details, which weren't important anyway. He knew who they were. He knew the settlers had run out of time.

The Piegans were coming and they would be out for blood.

Chapter Five

Nate counted 14 warriors. He shifted his gaze to the wagons and wildly waved his arm, motioning for the emigrants to head for the hill, but his effort was wasted. The men had climbed down and were conversing next to Webster's wagon. Not one noticed him. And only one of the women, Alice Banner, was in sight. She was idly staring off to the west, admiring the view.

"Damn greenhorns," Nate muttered, putting his heels to the stallion. Pegasus raced down the slope and across the flat. The Piegans were still out of sight to the south but they wouldn't be for long, and once the warriors spied the wagons they would rush forward to attack.

The men turned as he pounded up. Simon Banner was the first to notice the anger on his face. "What's the matter, King? You look like you're fit to be tied."

"Didn't any of you dunderheads think to keep an eye peeled on me?" Nate rejoined. "While you stand here jawing, the Piegans are closing the gap. I saw them from up yonder. We have to get to the top of that ridge just as fast as you can whip your teams."

They needed no further prompting. Dashing to their respective wagons, they hastily climbed up and started urging their teams toward the ridge. Banner was in the lead, as usual, his whip cracking the loudest, his bellowing the harshest.

Nate hung back to cover them. He focused on the point where he figured the war party would appear. Not quite a minute later it did, and as he had foreseen, the Indians bounded through the high grass like panthers rushing hapless prey, their shrill war whoops and bloodcurdling shrieks rending the air.

The wagons had reached the bottom of the ridge and the horses were now toiling up the slope. They strained in their harnesses, their muscles rippling, their backs straight, their heads bowed, as they threw their entire bodies into their work, the heavy wagons making difficult a chore they normally could achieve with ease.

Halting, Nate tucked the Hawken to his shoulder and pointed the heavy barrel at the onrushing Indians. They saw him but, in testimony to their courage, none of them slowed. He sighted on the fleetest of the band, a strapping warrior armed with a war club twice the size most men could wield. Cocking the hammer, he touched his finger to the cool trigger, held his breath, and verified the sights were right where they should be. Then, and only then, he lightly squeezed the trigger.

The Hawken cracked, belched smoke and lead, and the foremost Piegan did a somersault and disappeared in the grass.

Nate's fingers were a blur as he reloaded. First he fed black powder down the barrel. Then, using the ramrod, he shoved a patch and ball down until both were snug against the powder. Finally, he cocked the rifle again and took deliberate aim. This time he was thwarted, however, when the Piegans, to a man, went to ground. One moment they were speeding toward him; the next they were gone, seemingly vanished off the face of the earth.

Grabbing the reins, he goaded Pegasus up the slope, staying behind the last wagon all the way to the top. There, he dismounted and took a position above the spring. Below, the Piegans were fanning out. He caught glimpses of them here and there as they darted from cover to cover. Behind him drummed footsteps.

"What should we do?" Simon Banner asked.

"One of you take the north side, one the east, and one the south. If you get a good shot, try and cut the odds. If not, don't waste powder. And if you see them getting set to rush us, give a yell."

Neil Webster surveyed the barren acre. "I don't much like being hemmed in like this," he commented.

"You can't call this being hemmed in when we can make a run for it any time we want," Nate said. "This high ground gives us the advantage since we can see them before they get too close. And it's easier to shoot downhill than it is uphill."

"I still don't like it," Neil said.

Once they had moved off, Nate eased down among the boulders rimming the spring. He dipped his hand in the cold water and drank his fill, then crawled out to where he enjoyed a bird's-eye view of the whole west slope. A hundred yards off an Indian dashed from one tree to another, too quickly for Nate to snap off a shot.

What would the Piegans do? Nate wondered. They were crafty devils, and they were bound to realize that an assault from all sides at once would cost them too many men. Their best bet, and one they would see in no time, was to make a mass rush up a single side of the ridge, counting on their superior numbers to overwhelm the defenders.

Which side would it be? Nate's brow furrowed as he tried to think like a Piegan. The east slope, where the lightning-spawned fire had burned off the vegetation, was out of the question since the Piegans would be easy targets. Which left three possibilities. The south side, though, was connected to a neighboring mountain by a narrow shoulder with few trees and boulders. On the north the ridge sloped steeply down into a notch. So the best approach was from the west, the very slope Nate was watching.

He figured it would take the Piegans a half hour or better to work out their strategy, and he made himself comfortable. Crossing his arms, he rested his chin on his right wrist. Far to the west several buffalo were grazing. To the southwest soared an eagle. The serene scene belied what was taking place on the ridge.

Minutes passed slowly. He constantly scanned the slope, but saw nothing. His every instinct told him the Piegans were sneaking closer and closer, but for the life of him he couldn't spot them. Grudgingly, he had to admit they were every bit as skillful as the Blackfeet and the Bloods, whom he had fought more times than he cared to recollect.

"Mr. King?"

The softly uttered words startled Nate. He twisted, stunned to see Libbie Banner sliding down toward the spring, a tin cup gripped firmly in her left hand. "Don't—" he began, too late. For a heartbeat later there was a loud buzzing noise and a streaking shaft thudded into the earth within an inch of her left leg. To her credit, she didn't sit there paralyzed with fear. Instead, she scooted among the boulders and crouched low, her breaths coming in great gasps.

Nate checked the slope, saw no hint of the Piegans, and moved back to confront her. "What the blazes are you doing here? Are you trying to get yourself killed?"

"Ma got a fire going and whipped up a batch of coffee," Libbie said, holding out the cup. "She thought you might like some."

Of all the harebrained acts Nate had ever heard of or witnessed, this one took the cake. He was about to tear into her, to give her a piece of his mind for foolishly risking her life over a trifling cup of coffee, but he held his tongue. Both Alice and Libbie had the best of intentions. They probably believed they were helping out, doing what little they could in the crisis. Sighing, he took the cup. "Thanks. Just don't ever do this again. I don't want your death on my conscience."

Her response was unexpected. "Why should you care one way or the other if I live or die? You hardly know me."

"True," Nate admitted after taking a sip. "But I gave my word I'd see all of you folks safely to Fort Hall and I aim to do as I promised."

"I hope you won't be too upset if one of us doesn't make it."

"You?"

Libbie nodded. "As I told you before, I have no intention of reaching the Oregon Territory alive."

"Strange words coming from one so young. You have your whole life ahead of you. Why—"

"Please, don't," Libbie said brusquely. "I've heard all this already from my ma. The last thing I need is another long-winded speech about how I have so much to look forward to, and how I should be grateful to be alive."

Nate was surprised to learn that Alice knew how her daughter felt. It seemed to him that a girl would keep such a thing secret. "Does your father know you want to die?" he inquired.

Fleeting rage—or was it hatred?—rippled across Libbie's delicate features. "I would never tell him. He'd tan my hide good if he knew."

"A young lady your age is a bit too old to be spanked," Nate remarked.

"My pa doesn't think so. Until I marry, I'm his to do with as he pleases. And he's a firm believer in applying the rod of correction whenever I misbehave."

"Doesn't your mother object?"

"What Ma wants doesn't matter. In our family Pa rules. Every little thing has to be done just the way he wants or he sees red. If Ma objects, he slaps her around. He never talks things out. He treats us just like he does the horses." She paused. "No, I'm wrong. He treats his horses better than he does us."

"I'm sorry to hear that." Nate swallowed more coffee. "No woman deserves to be treated like property. When a man and a woman disagree, they should sit down and talk things out until they reach some common ground."

Libbie regarded him as she might someone from a foreign country. "Do you practice what you preach?"

"I try, but my wife isn't one for wearing her feelings on her sleeve. She keeps everything to herself, even when she's upset, so I have to pry things out of her. It tries my patience sometimes, I will confess. I'd much rather she'd come right out and speak her piece." Nate grinned. "Nicely, of course. No man can long abide being nagged."

"And you say I'm strange," Libbie said. "My ma told me that you're married to an Indian woman. And I've heard that Indian men treat their women about the same way my pa treats us."

"Not true," Nate said. "The men in different tribes treat their womenfolk differently. I'm an adopted Shoshone, and I can tell you from having lived with them off and on for years that the women in the tribe are always treated with respect."

"I had no idea. Too bad I wasn't born a . . ." Libbie began, and then her gaze strayed past him and her eyes became the size of saucers.

Furious at himself for being so stupidly careless, Nate whirled, sweeping the Hawken up as he turned. Two Piegans were at the boulders, the first in the act of drawing back his arm to hurl a lance. Nate fired from the hip. The ball smacked into the warrior's chest, dropping the man where he stood.

Undaunted, the second Piegan raised a tomahawk and charged, venting a nerve-tingling screech intended to freeze Nate in place.

Nate grabbed for a flintlock. His hand just touched the pistol when the Piegan reached him and the tomahawk arced at his head. Without thinking he threw himself to the right, and in so doing slammed his shoulder into a boulder. Pain coursed through his arm and down his spine. He tried once more to draw the flintlock but his right arm was temporarily numb.

Like a banshee the Piegan pounced.

From out of nowhere came a stream of dark fluid that struck the warrior in the face as he began to swing the tomahawk. Frantically the Piegan wiped his other forearm across his eyes to clear his sight.

That delay saved Nate's life. He drew the other flintlock, pointed it at the Indian's belly, and fired.

At such close range the ball staggered the warrior, sending him tottering backwards. Gurgling, the Piegan sank to his knees. In a last act of fierce desperation, he raised his tomahawk to throw it, but his strength failed him. His eyelids fluttered. He growled like an animal, then pitched onto his face in the dirt.

Nate scrambled up into a crouch. A glance at Libbie showed her holding the coffee tin he had dropped when he used the Hawken. Quickly he moved to the last boulder and peeked around it. Another pair of Piegans, evidently discouraged by the deaths of their fellows, were just seeking shelter behind pines lower down. He had a breather, and he used the time to reload his weapons.

The Piegans weren't pressing their attack. Perhaps, Nate reasoned, they had been probing to test the defenses of his small group. He hurriedly finished with the Hawken and began on the flintlock. Slight footfalls to his rear made him look over his shoulder.

"I've never seen anyone killed before," Libbie said weakly. "It's worse than I thought."

"It had to be done," Nate told her. "If I hadn't shot them, they'd now be taking our hair." He nodded at the top of the ridge. "You'd better sneak on back to the wagons. And tell your mother not to pass out any more coffee unless I say otherwise."

Libbie nodded. She glanced at the second Piegan he had slain, at the man's gut wound, and put a hand to her pale brow.

"Can you manage on your own?" Nate asked.

"I'm fine," Libbie said, but her dazed appearance made a mockery of the statement. She steadied herself against a boulder, then took a few steps.

"Hold up," Nate said, going to her side and taking her arm. "I'll escort you back." He disliked leaving his post, but he doubted she could safely scale the few feet of slope between the spring and the rim given her emotional turmoil. To those unaccustomed to the savage realities of frontier life, violent death could be extremely upsetting. Leading her to the boulder nearest the rim, he held her arm tight and suddenly burst from concealment, hauling her along with him.

An arrow whizzed from out of the blue and sank into the soil to their right.

Nate's back prickled until he was up and over and he had dropped flat. Libbie stayed close to him the whole time. Turning, he inched to the edge and peered down at the slope. The Piegans were still in hiding. But for how much longer?

Backing away, he took Libbie's hand and made for the wagons where the women were waiting. They had heard the shots, and all wore expressions of worry. Alice, her dress swirling about her ankles, ran to meet him halfway.

"What happened?"

"Two Piegans tried to jump us," Nate disclosed. "Your daughter is a bit rattled."

"The poor dear," Alice said, putting her arm around Libbie's shoulders. The girl stood docile, as blank as an empty slate. "As if she hasn't been through enough in the past few months." She led Libbie off. "I swear that if we make it to the Oregon Territory alive, I'll make it all up to her."

What did that mean? Nate reflected, and pivoted when Simon Banner and Neil Webster ran up to him. Before they could open their mouths, he tore into them. "Damn your hides! Don't any of you have the common sense God gave a turnip? How could you leave your positions at a time like this?"

"But we heard—" Simon tried to object."

"If the Indians were trying an all-out attack, I would have given a yell for your help," Nate declared. "And if they'd made it past me, you would have heard the women scream. Now you've left two sides undefended." He scanned the top of the ridge. "Where's Harry? At least he had the brains to stay put."

"He's on the north side," Simon said.

Nate looked in that direction, doubt creeping into his mind. Young Harry Nesmith was the hothead of the group, the rash one who always did things without thinking. It was odd that Nesmith should be the only man who hadn't come on the run upon hearing the shots. So odd, in fact, as to spark a disturbing premonition. He broke into a run, angling toward the north end of the ridge.

"What's the matter?" Simon asked.

"King, what's wrong?" Webster added.

Nate saved his breath for running. Shy of the edge he slowed and dropped into a crouch. On silent feet he moved to where he could see the upper portion of the notch and the slope below it. There was no movement, not so much as the flutter of a chipmunk's tail. Nor did he spy Nesmith. Lowering onto his elbows and knees, he carefully worked his way forward until his head poked over the edge. It was then he found the hothead.

Harry Nesmith lay on his back in a pool of blood between two huge boulders at the bottom of the notch. His blank eyes gazed lifelessly at the azure sky. Jutting from his chest were two deeply imbedded arrows.

Racked by guilt, Nate frowned and pulled away from the edge. He hadn't thought much of Nesmith, but he hadn't hated the man either. In any event, his personal feelings didn't really count. What did matter was his failure. He had promised to do his best to get all of the emigrants to Fort Hall, and now he had lost one of them.

Footsteps heralded the arrival of Simon Banner and Neil Webster, who both dropped flat.

"Where's Harry?" Simon inquired. "He should be right around here somewhere."

Nate jerked a thumb at the edge, then moved a few yards before standing and walking toward the wagons. His next chore weighed heavily on his heart. He would much rather face a horde of Blackfeet unarmed than do what had to be done. Eleanor Nesmith and Cora Webster were watching him approach, and he avoided meeting their anxious gazes until he was right in front of them.

"Something's wrong, isn't it?" Eleanor immediately asked. She stared northward. "Where's my Harry? Please don't tell me what I fear you're going to tell me."

Words were unnecessary. Nate merely looked at her, his sorrowful countenance conveying the message he couldn't bring his lips to utter.

"Oh, God!" Eleanor exclaimed, tears flowing from the corners of both eyes. "Dear Lord, no!" She spun, her hands covering her face, her shoulders quaking as she began sobbing uncontrollably.

"I'm sorry," Nate mumbled. Her grief was like a red-hot knife blade searing the core of his being. He felt as if he was directly to blame for the tragedy. Cora Webster put an arm around Eleanor. Overcome with remorse, not knowing what he could possibly say or do that would help, he moved to one side and bowed his head in thought.

He had to suppress his guilt and concentrate on their predicament or more lives would be lost. The Piegans were bound to attack soon. And with one man dead, defending all four sides of the ridge was now impossible.

"Mr. King?"

Nate looked around. Alice Banner was climbing down from the first wagon. "Yes?"

"Are we going to be moving out soon?"

"I don't rightly know yet. Why?"

"Libbie is in no shape to travel," Alice said, walking over. "She's just lying in there in a state of shock. All of this has been too much for her on top of everything else she's been through. She's so young, after all." A loud wail from Eleanor Nesmith caused her to stop and scowl. "I couldn't help but overhear about Harry. If you ask me, now we have two reasons to stay put for a while. Eleanor is in no condition for traveling either."

"We may not have much choice but to leave," Nate said.

"But if we do, who will drive the Nesmiths' wagon? Eleanor is too distraught."

"We'll figure that out in a bit," Nate said, scanning the ridge. The conversation had served to rouse him from his budding melancholy, and he realized he had better stop feeling sorry for what had happened and work to save the lives of the rest of the settlers. At the moment no one was keeping watch; the Piegans could be among them before they knew it. Hefting the Hawken, he ran to the west side and knelt near the rim. Below, a pebble or stone rattled loudly. He removed his hat, then rose up high enough to view the entire slope, and the moment he did a glittering shaft sped from behind a tree and nearly clipped his left ear.

Nate went prone and cocked the Hawken. Since the spring offered ideal protection and was their only source of water, he donned his hat once more and crawled close to the slope. He had to make a dash for the boulders and hope for the best. The Piegans had seen Libbie and him leave the spring, so the warriors might be expecting him or someone else to return. They would have the slope well covered.

Touching his left cheek to the grass, he slid out far enough for a quick glance. What he saw made him recoil in alarm. There were two Piegans at the spring! He glimpsed them crouched behind boulders. Now the Indians had control of the water supply, and any attempt to try and drive them off would result in certain death for some of the emigrants.

He heard a faint noise and risked another look-see. A Piegan was just disappearing behind a tree close to the spring. Others must have worked their way higher in his absence. Twisting, he saw Simon and Neil at the wagons and beckoned for them to hasten over. This time they were paying attention.

"What now?" Banner whispered when they got there.

"Spread out and get set. I have a hunch we're about to have some visitors," Nate said softly.

Neil Webster swallowed. "Shouldn't one of us stay with the women in case the savages make it over the top?"

"The women will have to fend for themselves. We'll be too busy," Nate predicted. As if on cue, a piercing war whoop sounded and was echoed by a dozen throats. He surged to his knees, aware they had run out of time and options, and beheld a ragged line of Piegans sweeping toward the crest. "Here they come!" he cried, wedging the stock of the Hawken against his shoulder. "Give them hell!"

Chapter Six

There were ten Piegans, all told, their painted features animated by the bitter hatred they bore all whites. Shrieking and waving their weapons, they bounded upward like agile mountain sheep. In their frenzied desire to count coup on their mortal enemies they paid no heed to their personal safety.

Nate took a bead on one of the pair rushing out from among the boulders bordering the spring. This time he went for a head shot, and his ball put a new hole smack between the Piegan's brown eyes. Lowering the Hawken, he heard Banner's and Webster's rifles crack as he whipped out a flintlock.

Arrows zipped past or arched overhead. He pointed the pistol at a charging warrior, then fired. The Piegan clasped his side, stumbled, and fell. To the left another Piegan had almost gained the top. Rising and taking four swift strides, Nate jammed the spent flintlock under his belt, grasped the rifle barrel with both hands, and swung the gun like a club.

The stock smashed into the Piegan's temple and the man toppled.

Yet another Piegan, lower down, whirled and ran.

Simon Banner and Neil Webster were embroiled in a life-and-death struggle with three warriors. Banner was using his gun in clublike fashion, holding two warriors at bay. Webster, however, was down, an arrow in his shoulder, grappling with a stocky Piegan who was trying to bash in his skull with a war club.

Nate sped to their aid, drawing his second flintlock en route. Without slowing he aimed at the stocky Piegan astride Webster and sent a ball crashing into the warrior's right ear. Then, discarding both the flint-lock and the Hawken, he drew his butcher knife and his tomahawk and closed on the pair striving to slay Banner.

One of the Indians glimpsed him coming and spun to meet him. A war club swept at his face.

Pivoting, Nate blocked the club with his tomahawk and in the very next instant buried his butcher knife in the Piegan's torso. The warrior grunted and buckled, his legs as weak as runny pudding. Taking a breath, Nate threw himself at the third Piegan. The Indian was so intent on killing Simon Banner that he didn't see Nate's tomahawk swing in a loop that ended with the keen edge shearing off the back of his head.

Spattered with gore and blood, Nate faced the slope. To his amazement, their determined resistance had blunted the attack and the surviving Piegans were in full flight. He counted three warriors, one holding a hand to a bloody head.

"Alice!" Simon suddenly shouted.

Nate whirled and was dismayed to discover two Piegans were at the wagons. While most of the war party had kept him and the others busy, those two must have snuck up on the women from another direction. One was wrestling

Alice on the ground, trying to subdue her by pinning her arms. The second warrior had seized Eleanor by the wrist and was attempting to drag her off. Cora Webster stood with her back against her wagon, rigid with overpowering fear.

"Reload your guns!" he yelled at Banner, and sprinted toward the conflict.

The Piegan struggling with Simon's wife looked up and saw him coming. Letting go of Alice, the warrior stood and unslung a bow that hung over his left shoulder. In a smooth, practiced motion the Piegan drew an arrow from a quiver on his back and nocked the shaft to the sinew string.

Nate knew there was no way he could reach the warrior before the Indian loosed that shaft, and he tensed his leg muscles in preparation for throwing himself to one side when the Piegan let it fly. But help came from an unexpected source. Libbie Banner abruptly appeared in the Banner wagon, rising behind the front seat, a pistol clutched in both hands. She trained the gun on the Piegan's back and fired.

Struck between the shoulder blades, the warrior was thrown forward by the force of the ball tearing through his body. He tripped over Alice and fell to his knees, his stunned gaze on the blood-rimmed exit hole in his chest.

In seconds Nate was there. He drove the tomahawk into the Piegan's forehead, splitting the man's brow wide open, and spun toward the warrior trying to haul off Eleanor Nesmith. The Piegan was glaring at him, and when he started toward them the warrior flashed a knife from a hip sheath and plunged the blade into Eleanor's bosom.

"No!" Nate cried. A rifle cracked behind him, but whoever fired missed. The Piegan, smirking in triumph, spun on his heels and ran for the west rim. Nate reached Eleanor's side as she collapsed and he caught her in his arms, staring aghast at the blood streaming from the knife wound. She tilted her head and locked her eyes on his, eyes eloquent with a mute appeal he would remember for the rest of his life.

Eleanor's lips parted. She tried to speak, but all that came out was an agonized groan. Stiffening, she grabbed at his buckskin shirt, her bloodstained fingers smearing red streaks on his chest. Her movements weakened. In desperation she sucked air into her lungs, then frantically attempted to stand. Her legs wouldn't cooperate. Eyes wet with moisture, she glanced again at Nate, mustered a partial smile, and died.

Another shot sounded. Nate looked up to see the last Piegan vanish over the crest. Simon Banner was the one who had fired, and he now trotted to the west rim and shook his fist in the air while calling down the wrath of the Lord on the savages. Nate barely heard the words. He gently lowered Eleanor to the grass, closed her open eyes, and stood.

"Is she dead?" Alice Banner asked, coming up on his right side.

"Afraid so," Nate said ruefully. "First her husband, now her." He refrained from adding that given the way things were going, more of the emigrants might lose their lives before they reached Fort Hall. They'd be lucky if any of them made it.

"We'll have to give them a proper Christian burial."

At any other time and place the innocent statement would have been thoroughly appropriate, but right then and there, on the heels of the frenetic battle they had just been through and with the hostiles likely lurking below, it struck Nate as so ridiculous that he inadvertently laughed and shook his head.

Alice was horrified. "Mr. King! What, sir, can be so humorous at a terrible time such as this? Surely not the deaths of two fine people? Eleanor was a sweet, gentle soul who never wished ill of anyone."

"I'm not making light of Eleanor's passing," Nate said, but before he could offer an explanation both Simon Banner and Neil Webster came up, Webster doubled over with a hand gripping the arrow in his shoulder.

"Oh, no!" Neil said plaintively, staring at Eleanor. "Not both of them! So much for their dream of owning a prosperous farm in the promised land."

Simon hardly gave the body a glance. "What will happen next, King? Have we convinced the savages that they should let us be? You said that if we killed enough of them the heathens would give up."

"I said they *might* leave us alone," Nate corrected him. "Their next move is anyone's guess."

"What do we do then?" Simon snapped. "Stay here and wait for them to make up their minds?"

"No," Nate said, reaching a decision. "We'll leave as soon as you and I plant Eleanor. We dare not expose ourselves trying to get Harry, so I'm afraid his body must be left for the vultures. Alice and Cora will dig the arrow out of Neil."

"You want us to do *what*?"Alice Banner blurted out. She glanced dubiously at the shaft and slowly shook her head. "I don't know as how we can do it. Neither of us have much medical experience, and we've certainly never extracted arrows or bullets. Why, I'm afraid I'd faint halfway through."

Nate suppressed his disappointment. He should have expected as much, given that these were women who had never had to contend with hostiles before. In a way, his own wife had spoiled him. Winona was so marvelously self-reliant that he unconsciously expected all other women to be equally as competent, which wasn't the case. She could do anything and everything essential to life in the wilderness; she could cook, sew, skin game, tend injuries, cure sickness, ride like the wind, and perform a hundred and one other tasks in expert fashion. She could even fight like a wildcat when the occasion demanded. Until that moment, he hadn't quite appreciated how perfect she was for him. "Very well," he said. "I'll take the arrow out myself."

"Thank you," Alice said. "I'll help my husband bury Eleanor."

Neil Webster had to be helped to the fire. Nate got Cora busy boiling water. She had to be shaken a few times to snap her out of the abject fright that had seized her when the Piegans struck, but once she came around she applied herself diligently to the chore. She also climbed into her wagon and brought out several clean cloths to use.

Nate made Neil lie on his right side. Unbuttoning the homespun shirt, which was soaked with blood, Nate drew his butcher knife and cut a straight line from the top button to the shaft. Next, he peeled back the drenched fabric so he could examine the wound. The arrow had transfixed a fleshy part of the inner shoulder, below the collarbone, and gone completely through Webster's body. The barbed tip extended four inches out of the emigrant's back. "You're a lucky man," Nate remarked.

"Lucky?" Neil said, and grunted when Nate touched the arrow. "How do you figure?"

"The tip didn't strike a bone and wedge fast, as some are prone to do. Getting them out is a real chore. More often than not they break off when you try," Nate said, talking to keep Webster's mind off of the impending operation. It would be easier to extract the shaft if the settler was somewhat relaxed. He leaned over to inspect where the arrow had poked out Webster's back. "A friend of mine by the name of Jim Bridger got a couple of arrows in the back once, courtesy of the Blackfeet. One came out easy enough, but the head of the second one was hooked on a bone. So Bridger carried that arrowhead inside of him for three years, until he met up with a surgeon who could take it out." He smiled at Neil. "You're a heap luckier. I'll have this shaft out in no time."

"What will you use?"

"This," Nate said, holding up his knife. Twisting, he thrust the blade into the fire, letting the flames get the steel good and hot.

"Oh, God," Neil whispered.

"You'll do fine," Nate said, hoping he was right. Few jobs were more nerve-racking than trying to remove an arrow from a squealing weakling who wouldn't lay still so the job could be done right. "From the look of things, this arrow didn't have any poison on it."

Neil blanched. "Poison?"

"Yep. Some Indians like to dip their arrowheads in snake venom or stick them into dead animals. One nick can make a man as sick as a dog. Or dead."

"I had no idea."

"Indians can be nasty devils when they want to be, but most of them are as decent as any white men who ever lived," Nate said, gazing at the west rim. Time was of the essence. The Piegans had taken a terrible beating and just might take it into their heads to make another try at killing the emigrants. By all rights he should be keeping an eye out for them, but he was the only one who could remove the arrow. And if it wasn't extracted soon and the wound cauterized, Neil Webster might bleed to death.

When the water was boiling, Nate gave instructions to Cora. She knelt and lifted her husband's head into her lap, then took his hands in hers. Nate dipped a cloth in the water, being careful not to burn himself, and gingerly wiped the skin clean around the arrow, both on the front and the back. Neil flinched but held up otherwise.

"All set?" Nate asked.

"Get it over with."

Working swiftly, Nate snapped the arrow in half several inches below the feathers. Then he moved behind Webster, braced his feet on Webster's hips, and used the tip of his butcher knife to open the exit hole a half inch. Placing the knife down, he gripped the shaft with both hands, bunched his arm and shoulder muscles, and pulled with all his strength. The arrow hardly budged. Again he tried, and this time the shaft slid out an inch. By twisting it back and forth, he was able to loosen the arrow enough to pull it out halfway.

Neil Webster buried his face in his wife's dress but didn't cry out. He did groan repeatedly, and he trembled violently every time the shaft was twisted.

"We're almost there," Nate puffed, applying his sinews once more. He could feel the arrow sliding through the emigrant's flesh as, a fraction of an inch at a time, it slowly came out. Beads of sweat dotted his forehead when at long last he held the slender, dripping shaft in his left hand.

"It's out!" Cora exclaimed, and leaned down to kiss Neil on the temple. "Mr. King did it!"

"We're not done yet," Nate said, casting the arrow to the ground. Retrieving his knife, he held the blade in the flames to reheat the steel. Then he squatted in front of Webster. "You might want to grit your teeth," he advised, and when the emigrant did so, he touched the blade to the hole. There was a hissing noise and the odor of burning flesh assailed his nostrils. Webster stiffened and vented a low sob. Quickly, Nate moved around behind him and cauterized the exit hole as well.

Neil passed out.

"My poor darling," Cora said tenderly, stroking his neck. "He did all right, didn't he?"

"Yes, ma'am," Nate replied, rising. He saw his Hawken and the flintlock he had dropped during the battle lying where they had fallen and went to reclaim them, reloading his other flintlock along the way. A glance to the north revealed Simon and Alice Banner completing a shallow grave for Eleanor Nesmith.

Where was Libbie? In all the excitement, and what with having to operate on Webster, he had forgotten all about her. He looked at the Banner wagon, where he had last seen her, but if she was in there she was lying low. Stopping to bend down and pick up his discarded guns, he glanced to the south, and was amazed to behold Libbie strolling along the rim, a pistol in her right hand.

"What the hell!" Nate declared. He ran toward her, scanning the slope below, afraid one of the Piegans would be unable to resist such a tempting target. "Libbie!" he shouted. "Get away from there!"

She paid no heed and kept on walking.

Furious, Nate covered the distance swiftly, his arms and legs pumping. He jammed the pistol under his belt beside the other one. Libbie heard him as he drew close and started to turn. Grabbing her shoulder, he rudely yanked her back from the edge. "What in the world are you trying to do, girl? Get yourself killed?"

Her face the picture of sweet innocence, Libbie grinned and nodded. "Something like that."

"I don't understand you," Nate said, letting go. "One minute you save my hide, the next you're waltzing around in the open as if you're just asking for the Piegans to turn you into a porcupine."

"No such luck," Libbie said, her grin replaced by a frown.

Exasperated, Nate checked the slope. "I don't know why you're so all-fired set on killing yourself, but I won't let you do it. Not so long as I'm the guide of this outfit."

"You can't stop me."

"I'll do whatever it takes. If need be, I'll have your father tie you up until we reach Fort Hall."

"Pa would never do a thing like that."

"If he loves you, he will."

Libbie's next words were barely audible. "There are different kinds of love, Mr. King. Some are good. Some are bad. My pa would never tie me up because he doesn't care whether I keep on breathing or not. To him I'm vermin."

"You're talking nonsense, girl. All decent parents love their children."

"Not quite true. All decent parents love *decent* children. And I don't happen to qualify."

"What—?" Nate said, but she had turned and was trotting to the wagons. Utterly confused, he availed himself of the momentary free time to load the Hawken and his other pistol. To his relief, the Piegans appeared to have gone. At least he didn't spot any.

The surviving emigrants were gathered at the fire when Nate returned. They looked expectantly at him, every face betraying anxiety except for Libbie's. She was too downcast to care about their dilemma.

"We have two choices," Nate began. "We can stick it out here until we're positive the Piegans have left, or we can hightail it now, before they think to regroup and try again."

"I say we depart immediately," Simon stated. "But what do we do about the Nesmith wagon? Simply leave it for the heathens to plunder?"

"No," Nate said. "I suppose we should take it with us to Fort Hall. From there we can arrange for a letter to be sent." He stared at each of them. "That is, if Harry or Eleanor ever mentioned their kin to you."

"A brother of Harry's lives in New Jersey," Simon said. "At Trenton, I believe."

Neil, who sported a fresh bandage and was holding his left arm tucked to his side, faced the Nesmith wagon. "Wanting to do the right thing is all well and good, but who is going to drive this thing? I can't, and Simon will be busy with his own wagon."

"I will," Nate offered. "We cut out in five minutes." He walked to Pegasus and brought the stallion over, then used a length of rope to tie the animal to the rear axle. A peek over the back loading gate revealed that the Nesmiths had brought everything they would need to start their new life in the Oregon Territory, and then some. A chest of drawers, a stove, and a plow were among the heavier items packed on the bottom of the wagon bed. On top had gone cooking utensils, clothes, flour, salt, a water keg, blankets, an ax, and much more, all packed neatly and strapped down to prevent slippage on the trail. He was inclined to toss out the plow and a few other big items to make the wagon lighter, but there wasn't time. The Piegans might surge over the crest at any second.

He climbed on the wagon, leaned the Hawken beside him on the seat, snatched up the traces, and released the brake. Turning to see how the emigrants were faring, he found all of them ready to go. Cora Webster was waiting expectantly for the word to be given, her wounded husband, his face as pale as a sheet, next to her.

"I'll go first," Nate announced. "Stay close. If the Piegans try to stop us, put your whip to your team and make for the flatland. If they press us, try to discourage them with a few shots."

"We know what to do," Simon Banner growled. "Let's get on with it, shall we?"

Nate urged his team into motion and slanted to the west slope. His experience with wagons was limited, and he hoped he wouldn't make a mistake that would cause the Nesmith wagon to flip over on the way down. He knew enough to keep it pointed straight at the base of the ridge and to be ready to use the brake lever should the speed become too great. But the seasoned horses knew their business and brought him safely to the bottom without mishap.

The Piegans were nowhere in evidence. He suspected the war party had fled into dense forest to the south, which was the nearest heavy cover, and he scoured the woods time and again but saw no one. Once in the high grass he cracked the whip a few times and headed due west. In two hours they would come on a stream where he intended to call a halt.

Not having slept for so long, and being hungry enough to devour an entire bull elk at one sitting, he found himself becoming drowsy after going a mile. From then on he had to struggle to stay awake, but it was a lost cause. The rolling movement of the wagon lulled him into a dreamy, tranquil state. His eyelids became leaden with fatigue. He dozed off, snapped awake when the wheels hit a rut, then dozed off again. He was on the verge of slipping into a deep slumber when Pegasus whinnied.

A man living in the wild learned to rely on his horse for early warnings of danger. With its keen hearing and scent, a horse was almost as dependable as a trained watchdog. Those mountain men who lived the longest were those who early on learned to sit up and take notice when their trusted animals neighed in alarm.

Nate intended to enjoy a long life. So when Pegasus whinnied, his head shot up and he shifted in his seat to gaze at the stallion, which was in turn gazing off to the southeast. Leaning to his left, past the canvas top, he scoured the stretch of open prairie on that side and to their rear. He could still see the ridge and the mountain chain of which it was a part. Other than a flock of sparrows winging their way to the north, all was still. Whatever had pricked the stallion's interest was either hiding in the grass or else too far off to be seen. But not too far off to be smelled, since a sluggish breeze was blowing from the southeast.

He shook his head to dispel tendrils of weariness plucking at his brain. There was a chance the Piegans were dogging the wagons, waiting for another opportunity to strike so they could take their revenge. It pained him to think that a guard would have to be posted when the wagons arrived at the stream because he knew who would have to stand the first watch.

Facing around, Nate cracked the whip. And saw the leading edge of a storm front sweeping in from the west.

Chapter Seven

The roiling black and gray clouds unleashed their full elemental fury minutes after Nate and the emigrants reached a thin strip of trees bordering the east side of the gurgling stream. He had pushed the weary teams as hard as he dared in the hope of reaching shelter, all the while watching the swirling mass overhead as the sun was blotted out and the blue sky was transformed into a crackling cauldron that had threatened to explode in a deluge at any moment.

When the rain came, it came in great driving sheets, mercilessly pounding the canvas covers and the exhausted horses. Lightning flashed on all sides. Thunder boomed, seemingly shaking the very ground.

Nate didn't bother to unhitch his team for the time being. They were better off right where they were instead of being tied to nearby limbs or brush since they couldn't bolt while in harness. If lightning struck close to the wagon, the worst they could do was shy and prance in fright. If they were tied to trees, they might panic, tear the rope loose, and flee. Then he would have to spend hours rounding them up. And too, he didn't relish the thought of being soaked to the skin.

So he grabbed the Hawken and climbed under the wagon top to wait out the storm. Made of hemp and water-proofed with linseed oil, the canvas cover kept out most of the rain. There was a drawstring at the bottom for closing the opening, and he promptly did so. Now only a few drops spattered in now and then.

Nate worked his way to the rear. Outside, high winds shrieked past, violently shaking the canvas. He looked out and found Pegasus standing flush with the wagon. Water ran from the stallion's mane and tail. It also ran down both sides of his saddle, which he had neglected to strip off.

"Of all the stupid . . ." Nate muttered, and set the Hawken down. Bracing himself, he swung over the loading gate and hurriedly removed the saddle and his gear, placing everything in the wagon. By the time he climbed back in, he was dripping wet.

The emigrants were all in their wagons. He saw Libbie peering out and waved, but she made no response. Drawing the rear string so that both ends of the canvas were now sealed off from Nature's fury, he settled down on a bundle of blankets and rested his head on a soft pillow. A few minutes of peace and quiet would be nice, he reflected, and began to plot the course they would take once the weather cooperated. But total exhaustion engulfed him.

Almost immediately he fell asleep.

A tremendous crash of thunder abruptly awakened him. Nate sat up, blinking in surprise, unsure of where he was or what he had been doing. His mind felt sluggish, his body sore. Shaking his head, he pushed to his knees. One look at the possessions piled high around him sparked his memory and he recalled everything. How long had he slept? he wondered. And why was it so much darker than it had been when he drifted off?

Nate moved to the back and loosened the draw string. The storm still raged, although with diminished intensity. Gloomy twilight blanketed the landscape, and he realized night was not far off. He had slept for hours! Annoyed, he glanced at the other wagons. Both were lit from within by lanterns, and vague shadowy silhouettes played across the canvas tops whenever someone moved. The emigrants were warm and cozy, which was more than could be said for him. His buckskins were still wet, his skin damp, and he shivered when a gust of wind struck him.

Locating a lantern, he lit it. Next he stripped off his buckskins and wrung them out. Hanging them up to dry took but moments, and then he wrapped himself in a blanket and squatted next to the lantern, which gave off considerable heat as well as light. In minutes he was comfortably warm.

His growling stomach prompted a search for food. Eleanor Nesmith had packed enough jerked meat and other foodstuffs to feed an army. Included were a half-dozen biscuits she had baked two days ago. He hesitated before taking a bite, thinking of that young, vibrant woman who had been so full of life when she baked the biscuits and who was now feeding the worms. Such was life. People never knew from one minute to the next when the Grim Reaper would claim them, so it made sense to live each moment to the fullest. What would be, would be, and no amount of fretting about it ever extended anyone's life a single second.

He greedily devoured the biscuits. Jerky rounded out his meal, and he washed it all down with gulps of cool water. Coffee would have been preferable, but building a fire would have to wait until the downpour ended.

Nate resigned himself to staying by the stream until morning. In a way, the storm had turned out to be a blessing in disguise. A night's rest would do wonders for all of them, especially the horses. Which reminded him. Reluctantly, he donned his damp buckskins and went out.

The rain had slackened to a drizzle, the wind had died to a whisper. Taking Pegasus first, he tethered the stallion close to the stream where both water and grass were readily available. Working rapidly, he unhitched the entire team and took all of them over. Then he walked to the Banner wagon, but discovered that Simon had already taken care of those animals. The Webster horses were still hitched, though, so he tended to them. Before going back to his wagon, he stepped up to the Webster's and called softly, "How are you doing in there?"

Cora appeared, her features downcast. "Neil has a fever, Mr. King. He's resting right now, bundled up so he'll stay warm. But I'm worried about infection setting in."

"Don't be. I cauterized the wound good and proper," Nate said. "A fever is common in cases like this. By morning it should break and your husband will be fine."

"I hope so."

Nate touched a hand to his hat and went back. As he passed the Banner wagon, a gruff voice hailed him.

"King! So you're the one I heard. I take it we're staying put for the night?"

"We are."

"How's Neil faring?" Simon asked.

"He'll pull through."

Banner twisted his head to survey the darkening sky. "What are the odds the Piegans will come after us?"

"I'd say they're pretty slim. The storm wiped out our tracks, so unless they were close behind us when it hit, they have no idea where we are," Nate said.

"Good riddance, I say," Simon declared. "I take it we'll leave at dawn?"

"We will," Nate confirmed.

"Good. Let's pray we don't run into any more hostiles." Banner looked to the right and the left, then shrugged and closed the canvas.

What was that all about? Nate reflected, stepping to his wagon and climbing up. As his leg slid over the top he saw a huddled figure in the corner. The lantern light glistened off her golden tresses and revealed the earnest expression she bestowed on him.

"Please, Mr. King, come in. I need to talk to you."

Puzzled, Nate sat down opposite her. "Do your folks know you're here?"

"No. Pa thinks I'm answering nature's call," Libbie said, and grinned at some private joke. "He won't expect me back for five minutes or so, which is plenty of time."

"For what?"

"For getting your opinion on something," Libbie replied, resting her elbows on her knees and her chin in her hands. "I've come to respect you. You're not the uncouth lout my pa thinks you are."

"He said that?"

"Not in so many words, but I can tell how he feels. He's not very pleased at having you be our guide. He thinks you're too young, that you don't know what you're doing. And he blames you for the loss of Harry and Eleanor. He told my ma that we had better watch you like a hawk from here on out to make certain you don't make any more mistakes."

To hide his anger, Nate bowed his head.

"But I figure he's wrong," Libbie went on. "My pa makes a habit of misjudging people, so don't be upset. I can tell that you're a man who knows what he's about. Everything you've told us so far has turned out to be right. And you know these mountains like I know the back of my hand." She paused. "It wasn't your fault the Piegans found us. Those things happen."

Nate waited for her to get to the point of her visit. He hoped it would shed some light on her strange behavior, on why she was so eager to die.

"Mr. King, how do you feel about killing?"

"In what way?" Nate asked, recalling the Piegan she had shot to save his life. Was that what this was about?

"In every way."

He leaned back and took off his hat. "When I first came out here from New York City, I was shocked by it. Indians kill whites. Whites kill Indians. Both kill animals. Animals kill other animals. So much killing was hard to take until I came to see that it's part of Nature's way." He put the hat down. "If a panther wants to live, it eats deer or whatever else it can catch. If an owl gets hungry, it eats a rabbit. If an Indian wants to count many coup and be considered a great man in his tribe, he has to go out and kill his enemies. It's all part of life in the wilderness."

"So you don't mind having to kill?"

"Not when there's a reason. I have to eat, like everyone else. So does my family. And as a husband and a father I have a duty to protect my wife, my son, and my own hide the best I'm able," Nate said. He patted the hilt of his butcher knife. "Out here, Libbie, only the strong survive. It sounds harsh, but that's the way of the world."

"How many men have you killed?"

"I haven't counted them."

"Ever killed white men?"

"A few," Nate admitted.

"And it doesn't bother you? You don't feel guilt? You don't feel as if you've committed a sin?"

For a young girl, she was posing difficult questions. Nate toyed with the fringe on his pant leg before answering. "I've thought about all that. Many times. I know the Bible says, 'Thou shalt not kill,' but look at Samson and David. They were both mighty warriors and they killed time and again. Yet they were close to God." He sighed. "Have I sinned by killing others who were trying to kill me? Maybe. I don't rightly know. But I do know I wouldn't be here today if I'd let them kill *me*."

"Have you ever killed a child?"

Shocked, Nate glanced at her. "Heavens, no! Shooting a hostile out for my hair is one thing. Murdering children is another."

"Would you if you had to?"

"No."

"How can you be so sure?"

There was something about her tone that gave Nate pause. She had leaned forward and her eyes were boring into him as if she was trying to see into the depths of his soul. "I can't think of any reason for killing a child," he said slowly. "Even the Blackfeet don't do it. They adopt young ones into their tribe."

Libbie started to speak, but a shout outside made her straighten and gaze anxiously at the darkness that had claimed the countryside.

"Daughter? Where are you? Your supper is getting cold!"

"I have to go," Libbie said urgently. She scooted to the front of the wagon, then hesitated. "Thanks for taking the time to hear me out. Maybe we'll talk again sometime."

"Whenever you want," Nate said, and watched her step onto the seat. Her legs coiled and she jumped from sight. He heard her clear her throat as she walked toward her wagon.

"Here I come, Pa! Sorry."

Peering over the loading gate, Nate saw Simon Banner waiting for her. Simon offered his hand, but she refused to take it and climbed up on her own. Perplexed, Nate tied the canvas and pondered. Why had she been so intensely interested in the killing of children? Had a younger brother or sister died some time ago and she was trying to come to grips with her grief? He wished they had not been interrupted so he could have gotten to the bottom of the mystery.

Another meal caused his drowsiness to return. He rearranged some of the Nesmiths' belongings so he had a flat space to stretch out, then spread the blankets and lay on his back. The rain had almost stopped. Far to the east thunder rumbled. He imagined that it must be raining on Harry Nesmith at that very minute, and regretted they had not had the time to bury the man beside his wife.

Presently he turned off the lantern, covered himself with two heavy blankets, closed his eyes, and drifted into a pleasant sleep.

Years of living in the wild had turned him into an early riser. There were only so many hours in a day, and if a man wanted to accomplish a lot he had to take advantage of daylight while it lasted. Thus it was that the faintest of pale tinges touched the eastern sky when Nate opened his eyes and stretched. The long rest had completely rejuvenated him. He jumped up, refreshed and eager to commence the day's work.

His buckskins were not quite fully dry, but they would be once he got outside and moved around. He dressed, aligned his weapons as they should be, snatched up the Hawken, and ventured out to check on the stock. All the horses were accounted for, right where they should be. He patted the stallion, then roamed among the trees in search of dry timber for a fire. It took some doing, but he soon had a blaze going.

The other wagons were still dark and silent. He moved quietly so as not to awaken them. After all the emigrants had been through, they deserved some extra rest. Taking a coffeepot and coffee from the Nesmith larder, he treated himself to a hot tin cup of the brew, adding a handful of sugar for sweetening. Sugar was a rare commodity in the mountains because the Indians never used it and the trappers could rarely afford it.

Gradually the world came alive. The horses moved to the stream to drink. Birds chirped in the trees, sparrows, chickadees, and jays all vying for the honor of the loudest singers. Ravens flapped overhead. A rabbit hopped into the open near the stream, but bounded off when one of the horses snorted.

Nate sipped his delicious coffee, warmed himself by the fire, and thought of how different life was in the mountains compared to the hectic existence of those who lived in the States. Here a man could take time to smell the roses, as Shakespeare McNair liked to say. He could relax and enjoy the natural wonders all around him. There was no one looking over his shoulder all the time, no one goading him to work harder or faster as had been the case when Nate worked as an aspiring accountant in New York City.

Here a man could take what life had to offer at his own pace, a luxury for those burdened souls back East who were constantly working more and more hours to make more and more money so they could have more and more things. His own father had been a case in point, laboring ungodly long hours six days a week so the family would prosper in a modest way. To think that he had once wanted to follow in his father's footsteps! Thank goodness his Uncle Zeke had invited him to come West, where he had discovered that there was more to life than making money— much more.

He finished his first cup of coffee, poured another. The horses were grazing. On the other side of the stream a doe stepped into the open, saw the horses, and ran off before he could grab the Hawken and fire. He heard a rustling sound behind him and pivoted on his heels.

Simon Banner, his hair disheveled, his expression that of a man not quite fully awake, was emerging. He gazed all around, then came toward the fire, scratching himself in various spots.

"Hello, King," he mumbled.

"Ready for a new day?" Nate asked.

"As ready as I'll ever be." Simon surveyed the trees. "Have you seen my daughter anywhere?"

"No."

"Where the hell has she gotten to this time?" Simon groused, and continued to the stream, where he knelt and splashed water on his face and ran his thick fingers through his hair.

Nate scanned the trees himself. With all of Libbie's crazy talk about wanting to die, he was concerned she might have taken her own life or simply wandered off to let Nature take its course. Then again, she might be tending to personal business. He swirled the coffee and downed the rest in large gulps.

"Still no sign of her?" Simon asked, returning from his ablution.

"Not yet."

"I swear that girl gets more contrary every day. Comes from having a sinful nature."

"Libbie?"

Simon nodded knowingly. "She seems all sugar and spice, but deep down that girl has a wicked streak a mile wide. Satan tempted her and she took the bait."

"I can't believe she's as wicked as you claim."

"That's because you don't know her like I do. You see the outside of a cup and think the inside is clean when it's not." Simon extended his hands close to the crackling flames. "I never thought I'd be saying this about my own flesh and blood; but Libbie is Satan's tool. If she would repent I could forgive her, but she won't."

Nate couldn't resist asking, "Is that why she's bitter toward you?"

"You've noticed? Ah, well, I should have expected as much," Simon said. "Yes, the girl despises me, and all because I try to live my life according to the Good Book. I'm stern, I know, but it's only to keep her on the straight and narrow. I don't want her to end her days in Hell."

"I doubt she will," Nate said to be cordial. "She has a good head on her shoulders. Eventually she'll marry a law-abiding man and raise you a passel of grandchildren to be proud of."

Surprisingly, Simon Banner turned beet red. "Maybe. But I doubt any God-fearing man will have her after what she's done."

"What did she do?"

Ignoring the question, Banner rubbed his hands together and turned away. "Now where in tarnation is that child?" He moved toward his wagon and shouted, "Libbie! Libbie, where are you?"

The yells were bound to awaken the others. About to chide Banner for being so inconsiderate, Nate changed his mind. It would soon be time to head out. He wanted to put as much distance behind them as possible before sunset. Not until then would he feel completely confident they had eluded the remaining Piegans.

"Libbie! Answer me!"

Nate stood and took the tin cup to his wagon. Placing it inside, he put a hand on his saddle, and was starting to lift it when a sharp cry rent the air.

"King! Come here, quick!"

Cradling the Hawken, Nate trotted to where Simon Banner was squatting well beyond the wagons, almost at the edge of the grass. "What did you find?"

"Take a look. Then you tell me."

The tracks were as plain as the nose on Nate's face, clearly embedded in the saturated soil. Four horses, two heavily laden judging by the depth of the hoofprints, had ridden up close to the camp from the east and a man had dismounted. Whoever it was had then approached the wagons but stopped ten feet off. Another set of footprints, smaller and dainty, undoubtedly those of a young woman, ran in a straight line from the Banner wagon to where the man had stood. Together the pair had stepped to the man's horse and mounted, and all the horses had made off to the southeast.

"Does this mean what I think it does? My daughter went with these strangers?"

Suddenly Nate remembered his encounter with the two greenhorns named Brian and Pudge at South Pass. In all the excitement of battling the Piegans, he had forgotten about them. But he would wager a year's catch of prime beaver pelts that the tracks in front of him were left by the pair and their animals.

The shouts had drawn the rest of the emigrants. Alice had a green shawl wrapped around her shoulders. Neil Webster was pale but held himself erect, Cora supporting him with an arm around his waist.

"Libbie has been kidnapped!" Alice now declared in stark horror. "Did the savages take her?"

"No, these were shod horses. Even I can see that," Simon answered, and glanced up at Nate. "Say, you never did tell us who had that fire going on the top of South Pass. Could they be the ones who took our girl?"

"There were two of them," Nate said. "Called themselves Brian and Pudge."

"Oh, God!" Alice wailed. "Not him!"

Glowering in unbridled rage, Simon rose and shook a fist at Nate. "Why didn't you tell us about them sooner? Do you have any idea what you've done, you fool?"

"If you'll recall," Nate said, keeping his temper with a monumental effort, "the minute I got back to camp, I had to stop some of the Piegans from stealing your stock. From then on we were kept busy just staying alive." He shrugged. "I forgot about Brian and Pudge."

"Of all the dunderheads who ever lived, you take the cake!" Simon practically roared. "Now, thanks to you, our daughter has been taken by those degenerates." Taking a step, he drew back his fist. "I should thrash you within an inch of your life."

And with that, Simon swung.

Chapter Eight

Nate exploded, releasing his pent-up feelings in a burst of fiery indignation. For days the emigrant leader had treated him as less than dirt, insulting him, mocking him, taunting him, and he had tolerated all he was going to stand. He blocked Simon's swing with the Hawken barrel, then rammed his right fist into Simon's mouth. Banner's lips split wide and the emigrant staggered. Unrelenting, Nate stepped in and landed a blow on Simon's cheek, then buried his fist in Simon's stomach.

"Stop it!" Alice screamed. "Please!"

Not in any mood to slack off, Nate delivered a sweeping punch to the chin that straightened Banner like a board. Slowly Simon crumpled into a limp heap, blood dribbling from his smashed mouth.

"How could you?" Alice yelled at Nate. She knelt beside her husband and tenderly took Simon's head in her hands. "Look at what you've done to him! And I thought you were a decent man!"

"I suppose you'd be happier if he had pounded me to a pulp?" Nate responded in disgust. Hefting the Hawken, he whirled and went to the horses. It would be a cold day in Hell, he mentally vowed, before he took a job as a guide again. Easterners had no respect for anyone but themselves, a fact he should have remembered form his years in New York. He led Pegasus to the back of the Nesmith wagon, leaned his rifle against a wheel, and hurriedly saddled up. After filling a parfleche with jerky, he rolled it in a blanket and tied both behind his saddle. As he gripped the reins to mount, he heard footsteps.

"Where are you going?" Neil Webster asked.

Nate swung up, then leaned down to scoop up the Hawken. "Where do you think?" he rejoined. "Someone has to fetch the girl back."

Cora exhaled in relief. "We were afraid you were leaving us to fend for ourselves." She forced a smile. "Not that we'd blame you after the way some of us have been treating you."

"I took the job of escorting all of you to Fort Hall, and that's what I aim to do," Nate said. He nodded at the Banners. "Do what you can to calm them down. And make damn sure that none of you try to follow me. I should be back by dark, but if I'm not, don't fret."

"Take care of yourself," Neil offered.

"Always," Nate replied, touching his heels to the stallion. Was their concern genuine, or were they only worried about what would happen to them if he failed to come back? He rode past the Banners and Alice turned spite-filled eyes on him, but she made no comment. Simon still lay unconscious.

Angling to the southeast, Nate stuck to the fresh tracks. His blood still raced, his temples pounded, and he was glad to be on the go again, to be doing something that would take his mind off the emigrants. Being away from them for a spell was just what he needed.

He stared at the tracks, concentrating on the task at hand. Brian and Pudge must have reached the stream in the wee hours of the morning, well after the rain had ended, since there was no water in any of the hoofprints, so they couldn't have more than a two-or three-hour lead. Burdened as they were with two pack animals, and with one of them riding double with Libbie, they should be easy to overtake.

Pegasus enjoyed being given free rein, and ate up the distance at a steady trot. Other than a few antelope and a solitary hawk, nothing else moved in the great basin between the Wind River Range and the Salt River Range.

The golden sun cleared the eastern horizon, bathing the landscape with warmth and light.

Nate speculated on the connection between Libbie Banner and the two men she was with. From the tracks, he gathered she has gone with them willingly and not been kidnapped as her parents claimed. There had been no evidence of a struggle, no sign of scuffed, distorted footprints as there would have been had Libbie put up a fight. Nor had she bothered to call out. So she must know one or both of them.

An hour out from the camp he was disturbed to find that Brian and Pudge had changed direction. Now they were going due east. Why? Doing so would take them into the Wind River Range, where the Piegans were most active. Worse, if they continued on the way they were going, they would soon be near the very ridge where the emigrants had fought the war party. Should the surviving warriors still be in the area, the three whites would be in grave jeopardy.

He brought the stallion to a gallop and pressed on until the range appeared. Then he slowed to give Pegasus a brief rest, fastening his gaze on the point far ahead where the tracks blended into the grass in the hope of spotting the four horses and their riders.

The ridge became visible, half a mile to the north. He rode faster, the Hawken resting on his thighs, one hand on the rifle with his thumb on the hammer. Perhaps Brian and Pudge, knowing that someone would come after them, were heading for the forest covering the high slopes with the intention of losing themselves in the dense trees.

The trail brought him to the base of a foothill fronting a majestic peak covered with glistening snow. He stopped to scour the pines and boulders above. Suddenly he caught the unmistakable scent of smoke and spied a thin gray tendril wafting skyward halfway up the hill. They had stopped and made camp!

Grinning, Nate moved toward the spot. He would have Libbie back with her folks by mid-afternoon. Bending low, he passed under a thick limb, then went around a cluster of boulders. Of its own accord the stallion halted and tossed its head from side to side while uttering a low whinny.

Something was wrong.

Nate climbed down, tied the reins to a bush, and stalked upward. A clearing came into sight. In the center was the fire, or the embers of one, glowing red and giving off the smoke that had caught his eye. Not a living soul could be seen, nor were the horses anywhere nearby. Had they spotted him and left? he wondered, creeping nearer. Or had they only stopped for a short while, just long enough to grab a bite to eat, and then gone on?

Disappointed, he made a partial circuit of the clearing before he ventured into the open. In the soft earth at the base of a tree he discovered a moccasin print, and in the clearing itself, not a yard from the fire, was a puddle of moist blood. His worst fear had come true.

A thorough search revealed that four Piegans had surrounded the camp, then pounced at an opportune moment. One of the whites, Pudge by the footprints, had gone down almost immediately, but Brian had resisted mightily before being overpowered. The Piegans would have struck so fast that it was doubtful either of them had managed to get off a shot.

He found where the Piegans had headed to the northeast, leading the horses. Evidently Libbie was mounted, but the two men had been compelled to walk behind the animals with a Piegan trailing and probably covering them with a gun or a bow. Drops of blood confirmed that one of them was wounded. If he had to guess, he would say it was Brian.

Sprinting to Pegasus, Nate mounted and rode in pursuit. He was an hour behind the war party at the most, and on horseback he should come on them before noon. Heedless of the limbs that tugged at his clothing and scratched his face, he held the stallion to a brisk clip.

He felt reasonably certain the Piegans wouldn't slay their captives right off. The whites would be taken to the Piegan village, where the men would be tortured before being killed and Libbie would in all likelihood find herself the unwilling mate of a prominent warrior, unless the Blackfeet women got their hands on her first.

It had taken Nate a long time to come to terms with the Indian way of measuring manhood and gauging courage in their enemies. Torture was the preferred means. Mutilation of captives was widespread, not due to a depraved desire to inflict suffering but as a means of putting a captive to the supreme test. If an enemy held up stoically under the worst treatment conceivable, then that enemy was regarded as truly brave and a credit to his tribe and would be put out of his misery quickly. But if a captured foe whined and pleaded and groveled, then he was mocked and scorned and allowed to linger in the most intense agony for as long as he endured the ordeal.

Not all tribes resorted to the barbaric practice. The Shoshones, Nate's adopted people, were less prone to mutilation than most of the surrounding tribes, but they would unhesitatingly torture any Blackfeet, Bloods, or Piegans they caught. With perfect justification, because those three tribes were the very worst offenders of all the Indians living in the northern Rockies and Plains. Shoshones who fell into their hands knew exactly what horrors to expect, which explained why the Shoshones as a people were utterly merciless toward those three tribes.

The tracks took Nate up and over the hill, down into a ribbon of a valley, and then toward rugged mountains. Occasionally he came on more drops of blood, but they were fewer and farther between. Which was a good sign. If whoever had been wounded collapsed and was unable to go on, the Piegans would dispatch him then and there after testing his manhood in some diabolically gruesome manner.

At the base of a towering peak the trail turned northward. Nate was thankful for the recent storm. The rain-saturated soil bore clear prints, so tracking was a simple chore.

A mile further on the Piegans had turned to the northeast again, passing between two mountains on a well-used game trail. Indians knew that animals invariably followed the path of least resistance when traveling, making game trails ideal avenues for crossing rough terrain. The trappers had readily learned the same thing, and experienced mountaineers relied heavily on such trails when exploring new country.

There was another reason for the practice. Often game trails led to water, and water was precious to man and beast alike. Nothing lasted long without it. The man who stuck to a deer or elk trail could be confident that somewhere along the way there would be good drinking water.

Nate saw elk, deer, and mountain sheep tracks as he rode. There were also prints of smaller animals, such as rabbits, skunks, and porcupines. Mixed in with the tracks of the plant-eaters were the distinctive paw prints of panthers and bobcats. Because of the great number, he figured there was a lake or a river ahead.

His hunch proved correct.

Beyond the mountains unfolded a virgin valley lush with spruce, fir, and aspen trees. Dominating the center of the valley was a shimmering blue lake, toward which the game trail meandered through the underbrush. A carpet of pine needles muffled the thud of the stallion's hoofs.

Nate rode cautiously, his sixth sense telling him the Piegans were not far off. As he drew near the lake he heard gruff voices speaking in an Indian tongue he did not know. Halting, he slid down and worked his way along until he could see the lake and the shore clearly. There he found those he was after.

Three of the four Piegans were standing near the water, talking. The fourth, armed with a rifle taken from Brian or Pudge, stood guard over the captives. The two men and Libbie all had their hands bound behind their backs and were seated on the ground close to the horses. A large red stain on Brian's right shoulder confirmed he was the one who had been wounded earlier.

Lying down, Nate took aim at the Piegan holding the rifle. Then he paused, debating whether he should shoot. There was no chance of missing, but could he drop the rest of the Piegans fast enough to prevent any of them from reaching the three whites? The answer was no. And he wouldn't put it past the Piegans to use the captives as shields, or else to kill them out of blatant spite.

Reluctantly, he held his fire. He must await a better time. If some of the Piegans should go off to hunt or leave for some other reason, he would have the captives freed in no time. If he had to, he'd wait until dark, until most of the warriors were asleep, and then make his move.

At that moment Brian spoke. "Would it hurt to give us some water, you bastards?"

None of the Piegans paid him the least regard. The one acting as guard was gazing off to the north.

"Water!" Brian snapped. "We're all thirsty." He nodded at the lake. "All we want is a few sips. Is that too much to ask?"

The guard looked at him but made no response.

"At least let *her* have some," Brian persisted, indicating Libbie. "She's a woman, you savages! She deserves to be treated decently."

"You're wasting your breath," Pudge said softly.

"If I could only get my hands free," Brian said, straining against the rope around his wrists. His face became scarlet from his exertion and his veins bulged.

"Please don't," Libbie said. "You'll start bleeding again, and you've already lost too much blood as it is."

"I feel fine."

"You're a terrible liar. No man can take a knife in the shoulder and then act as if nothing happened. You should be resting comfortably in bed." Libbie glanced at the Piegans by the lake. "If they keep on pushing us as hard as they've been doing, all of us will be worn to a frazzle when we get to wherever we're going. But you'll be the worst off. So please, for my sake, conserve your strength."

"For you, dearest, anything," Brian said with a smile.

Nate's eyes narrowed. Had he heard correctly? Had the greenhorn just called Libbie his "dearest"?

"Don't say that," she replied. "It's my fault you're in this fix. If you hadn't come after me, we wouldn't be staring death in the face." She sadly shook her head. "You should have left well enough alone."

"Oh?" Brian said sarcastically. "I should have stayed back in the States while the woman I love was being taken against her will to the Oregon Territory? I should have let your father have his way when we both know he's wrong? When we both know that what he did was the most vile thing any person has ever done?"

Libbie closed her eyes, her mouth curling downward. "I don't want to talk about that."

"You must come to terms with it one day. Better now than ten years from now. It's enough to drive someone insane."

"Brian!"

Brian studied her tormented features, then scowled. "I'm sorry," he said, "but I can't help how I feel. If it wasn't for you, I'd put a ball in your father's head."

Tears poured down Libbie's cheeks and she doubled over as if in pain, her forehead resting on the grass.

Pudge angrily stared at Brian. "Now look at what you've done! Why must you upset her so at a time like this? Hasn't she been through enough already?" He made a clucking sound in reproach. "You're my best friend, so believe me when I say that sometimes you act as bad as these lousy Injuns."

The captives fell into a moody silence. Nate watched them, trying to piece together the little information he had gleaned. Now he understood why Libbie had gone willingly with the pair. From the sound of things, her father had nipped her romance with Brian in the bud and dragged her off to the promised land despite her wishes.

He saw the three Piegans walk over to the fourth, and after a brief discussion the captives were hauled to their feet. Libbie was bodily lifted onto a horse, the tallest of the warriors climbed on the other mount, and presently they were all moving around the west side of the lake. One of the Piegans handled the packhorses while the other two walked on either side of Brian and Pudge.

Nate ran to Pegasus and followed. He stayed in the trees, always keeping the party in sight but never, ever exposing himself to their view. Miles of forest fell behind them. The sun climbed ever higher. He wasn't worried that the Piegans would reach their village before nightfall since Piegan territory lay two or three days to the north-east, which would allow him plenty of time to effect a rescue.

He *was* worried, though, about the Banners and the Websters. Left long on their own, they might get into trouble. A fire built too big or random shooting was all it would take to attract any Indians within miles of their camp. And being as close to the stream as they were was also a danger since hostiles might decide to swing by for some water. To put his mind at ease he had to free Libbie and her friends that very night and try to be back at the wagons by early the next day.

The Piegans had ascended a rise and were now going down the far side.

Nate waited a few minutes to be on the safe side, then rode to near the top and slid down. Letting the reins drag, he moved to the top and slowly raised his head high enough to see the land below. What he saw about gave him a fit.

The party he was trailing had stopped in a meadow one hundred yards away. All of the Piegans were waving their arms and whooping and laughing at 12 *more* Piegans approaching from the south. This new group was likewise excited by the meeting, and soon the newcomers reached the meadow, where much hugging and smiling took place. The newcomers then turned their attention to the captives, some stroking Libbie's golden hair while others prodded and pushed Brian and Pudge. Brian flew into a rage and kicked one of those baiting him, at which point he was rendered unconscious by a war club to the back of his head.

Sinking down on his haunches, Nate rested his chin on his knees and felt a wave of helplessness wash over him. Saving Libbie and the greenhorns from four Piegans would have been difficult enough; saving them from 16 would be next to impossible. But he wasn't about to give up. As his mentor, Shakespeare, was so fond of repeating, "Where there's a will, there's a way."

Only in this case, the way eluded him. Sneaking into the Piegan camp after dark, after most of the warriors dozed off, was certain suicide. The Piegans would be doubly alert since they were in the wild where an enemy might discover them at any time, and a single light sleeper would prove his downfall. He must come up with a better plan.

Crawling back up, he watched the Piegans tie Brian's arms and legs to a long pole, which two of the stoutest warriors then carried between them as the combined bands hiked in the direction of their own country. Pudge was ringed by men with lances who delighted in jabbing him every so often. Libbie, placed back on her horse, was momentarily spared further indignities.

Nate went to Pegasus. There was nothing he could do for the time being except stay close and pray for a miracle. Instead of going over the top of the rise, where he was bound to be spotted, he rode to the left down the slope, entered the trees at the bottom, then adopted a course parallel with that taken by the Piegans. Bolstered by their combined numbers and elated at the spoils they were bringing back to their people, they were making enough noise to scare off every animal within half a mile. Laughter and singing carried on the wind.

The shadows lengthened as the sun banked toward the western horizon. Occasionally Nate caught glimpses of the war party, but for the most part he relied on his ears to mark their progress. The proximity of so many humans had silenced the wildlife; for over an hour he didn't hear so much as the peep of a bird.

A mountain crowned with two peaks jutting skyward like the twin horns of a bull turned out to be the Piegans' destination for the day. A sparkling creek bordered its base, and on the near bank the Piegans pitched their camp. The majority erected five conical log and brush forts, a customary practice of their tribe and their allies when on the trail, while several went off after game.

From under the sheltering branches of an overhanging pine, shielded by limbs that drooped to within a foot of the ground, Nate observed everything the Piegans did. The hunters had marched to the south, so he need not fear discovery by them. He saw Libbie, Brian, and Pudge shoved into a fort close to the creek, which gave birth to a daring idea.

Twilight claimed the mountains when the hunters returned bearing a large black-tailed buck. The deer was butchered by a skilled Piegan who took five minutes to do what would take the average trapper half an hour to accomplish. Presently they were all gathered around the fire to take part in the feast, except for a lone warrior who stayed in front of the conical fort containing the captives.

Nate crawled to where he had hidden Pegasus in thick undergrowth. He wedged the Hawken into his bedroll for safekeeping, then drew his tomahawk and his butcher knife and returned to his vantage point. The darkness deepened. The sun sank beyond the far mountains. In the rosy glow of the fire the faces of the Piegans gleamed dully.

He imagined they were doing as the Shoshones would be doing under similar circumstances, swapping tales of their exploits since leaving their village. The four who had survived the battle with the emigrants had a lot to tell, so he wasn't at all surprised when their conversation dragged on until almost midnight.

At last the Piegans began turning in. Only a few, at first, went into the forts. Then a few more. And so it went until all of them were inside save one who had taken the place of the man who had stood guard over the captives since sunset. Left unattended, the fire dwindled to low, sputtering flames.

Nate let more time pass before crawling from under the pine to the bank of the creek. Taking a breath, he eased into the shallow water, shuddering in the sudden cold, and turned toward the encampment. Just as he did, the Piegan on guard looked in his direction.

Chapter Nine

Nate froze in place, the gently flowing water soaking the front of his buckskins from his neck to his moccasins. Had the Piegan somehow heard him? He doubted it, since he had made no noise whatsoever. Holding the butcher knife and the tomahawk close to the water, he watched the Piegan scan the forest. The man didn't act as if he suspected there was an enemy about. On the contrary, after a minute the Piegan stretched and yawned, then strolled to the stream and knelt to drink.

Thirty yards away, Nate fought off an impulse to shiver and waited for the guard to move back to the fort. The creek, fed by snow runoff from the high peaks above, was liquid ice. Staying in the water too long would render his arms and legs numb. He would have no chance of freeing the others.

Finished quenching his thirst, the Piegan stood, wiped his mouth with the back of his hand, and walked back to the conical fort. He took up a position in front of it, then sat down with his legs crossed, his back to the fort.

Nate snaked forward, keeping his weapons above the water, using his elbows and his knees to propel himself, moving first one limb, then the other. The fire was now so low that its feeble glow bathed only the nearest forts. The one containing the captives stood shrouded in shadows.

He dared not go too fast for fear of making a splash that would be heard by the guard, yet he dared not dally either, or the cold would take its toll on his circulation. Hugging the near bank where the darkness was heaviest, he drew within ten yards of his goal.

The Piegan had set down his lance and had rested his elbows on his knees. He appeared bored, and was having trouble staying awake. Now and then his head bobbed, but he drew himself up again each time.

Nate stopped directly behind the fort where the three whites were held. Like an enormous salamander crawling onto land, he inched onto dry ground and paused to let the water run off his clothing. Warily, silently, he moved to the rear of the fort, then rose into a crouch. Gingerly taking a step, he moved to the right until he could see the back of the guard.

The rest of the camp was deceptively still. Should the guard sound the alarm, the Piegans would pour from the structures armed to the teeth and ready to fight to the death. From within a fort to the right arose loud snoring.

He glided toward the guard, his right hand firmly gripping the tomahawk. A single blow should suffice if delivered to the proper point. He saw the Indian's shoulders droop, took another step. The warrior was almost asleep. Raising the tomahawk overhead, he lifted a leg and carefully placed his foot down.

A twig snapped.

Muffled by Nate's wet moccasin, the snap was barely audible. But it caused the Piegan to jerk his head up and around, his right hand streaking for the lance by his side.

Nate was braced and ready. As the warrior turned, he swung, driving the tomahawk downward with all the power in his arm. The sharp blade bit into the Piegan's forehead above the right eye and split his skull like an overripe melon, burying itself inches deep in his head. Blood spurted. The Piegan gasped, clutched at the tomahawk, then broke into violent convulsions.

Nate held onto the tomahawk handle with both hands. Afraid the thrashing would awaken some of the other warriors, he glanced at the closest forts. The guard's arms went suddenly limp, then the man slumped forward, his eyes locked wide, his mouth contorted in a grimace.

Satisfied the guard was dead, Nate put a foot on the Piegan's shoulder and wrenched the tomahawk loose. He wiped the blade on the Indian's leggings, then padded to the fort and squatted in the opening. Inside lay three inky forms. Entering, he moved to Libbie, conspicuous by her long blond hair even in the gloom. From the way she was lying, he gathered her ankles and wrists were bound.

"I saw what you just did, mister," she abruptly whispered. "You look vaguely familiar. You are a white man, aren't you?"

"It's Nate King. I've come to free you."

A startled exclamation burst from the figure on the left. "Thank God!" Pudge declared. "I thought we—"

Nate reached the greenhorn in a single stride and clamped a hand over Pudge's mouth, gouging the hilt of his knife into the man's lips in the process. "You damn fool!" he snapped. "Do you want to set the Piegans on us?"

Pudge, the whites of his eyes the size of walnuts, vigorously shook his head.

Nate listened intently but heard nothing to indicate any of the warriors had heard. "I want all of you to keep quiet," he directed softly, releasing his hold on the greenhorn. "When I cut you loose, don't make a sound." Moving behind them, he quickly sliced through the ropes. They rose to their knees, all three rubbing their wrists and ankles to get their blood flowing again.

Outside, an owl hooted.

Edging to the opening, Nate surveyed the forts. Had that been a real owl or a signal? With Indians it was hard to tell. Some of them were so expert at imitating animals that it was impossible to know which was the real thing and which was not. He detected no movement. Twisting, he regarded Libbie and the two men. "We're going to try and reach the trees without being discovered. When you go out the entrance, turn to the right until you're at the creek. We'll follow it north into the woods."

For the first time Brian spoke. "What about our horses?"

"They're on the south side of the camp. I'll swing around and get them after all of you are safe."

"I don't like leaving them. Without our horses we wouldn't last a day in these mountains."

"Just do as I say and you'll come out of this still wearing your scalps," Nate said. He went out first, crouched until certain it was safe, then motioned for the others to emerge. Pudge was the last, and he grunted as he squeezed through.

His face reflecting his anger, Nate touched the keen point of his butcher knife to the heavyset man's fleshy cheek. Pudge blinked, then nodded his head once in understanding. Frowning, Nate gestured for them to move around the fort. He trailed them, keeping watch on the other log structures. The fire, now mere fingers of flame, revealed very little.

Instead of wading into the creek, Nate stuck to the water's edge. He was afraid one of them—most likely the clumsy Pudge—would inadvertently splash around or slip on a wet rock and arouse the war party. The soil bordering the creek was soft, cushioning their footfalls nicely, and soon they were in the sheltering forest where he halted.

"My horse isn't far," he disclosed. "I'll take you to him, then go after your own animals."

"How did you find us?" Libbie asked. "How did you know we'd been captured?" She paused. "Did my father send you?"

"We'll talk about that later," Nate said, and rose to head for Pegasus. A hand fell on his shoulder.

"Our supplies, King," Brian said. "I saw the savages remove our packs. We have to get them back."

Nate had witnessed the same thing. "The Piegans put all of your equipment in one of their forts. We have no hope of sneaking in there and getting it out, so you'll just have to make do."

"Without food? Without weapons? What chance will we have to survive in this wilderness?"

"You should have thought of that before you left the settlements. These mountains are no place for greenhorns," Nate responded, and shrugged to dislodge the man's hand. He hurried through the underbrush until he came on the stallion, whispering to it as he approached so the horse wouldn't spook or whinny.

"Can I talk now?" Pudge asked.

"Go ahead," Nate said.

"I'm in your debt, King. I don't know how I can ever repay you, but I will someday. I swear it. If not for you, we'd all be goners."

"You have my thanks too," Brian said, but without a trace of heartfelt warmth or conviction.

Puzzled by the man's bitter attitude, Nate slid his knife into its sheath and tucked the tomahawk under his belt. If the situation was reversed, he'd be overjoyed at being saved from certain death. Brian, oddly enough, seemed to resent what had happened. Nate decided to get to the bottom of the matter later, after they had put enough miles behind them for them to be truly safe.

Removing the Hawken from the bedroll, Nate held the rifle in the crook of his left elbow and grasped the reins in his right hand. "Try not to make much noise if you can help it," he advised, casting a meaningful look at Pudge, and hiked to the southwest.

"I thought you were going after our horses," Brian said.

"I will, once we're due west of the Piegans."

"What difference does that make?"

"If something goes wrong, I don't want to have to swing around the Piegan camp to make good our escape. I want to be able to cut right out. And west is the direction we have to go to take Libbie back to her folks."

"Oh."

They covered ten yards in silence. Then Brian commented starchily, "If you were a gentleman, King, you'd let Libbie ride your horse. Or don't good manners count for much in these stinking mountains of yours?"

"Brian, what has gotten into you? How can you talk to Mr. King like that?" Libbie upbraided him.

"It's all right," Nate said to forestall an argument. "He has a point. But my stallion has become a contrary cuss and won't hardly let anyone ride him but me. Not even my wife, who has a way with animals. If I tried to put Libbie on him, he might make a ruckus the Piegans would hear."

"*You're* married?" Brian asked.

"Of course. Why are you so surprised?"

"Is your wife a white woman or a squaw?"

Nate stopped abruptly and whirled. Unconsciously, he leveled the Hawken. "I would be extremely careful were I you," he said coldly. "I won't abide anyone insulting my wife. The last man who did is dead."

The others resembled statues. Brian stared at the rifle barrel for a few seconds, then smiled wanly. "I meant no disrespect," he said softly. "After all that's happened, I guess I'm not my normal self."

"Please, Mr. King," Libbie chimed in. "I know Brian as well as I do myself. He doesn't hate all Injuns like some men do. And he doesn't make a habit of going around insulting people."

"That's nice to know," Nate said dryly. He resumed walking, and speculated on what would happen when they rejoined Libbie's parents. Simon wasn't the type to forgive and forget. The girl and her friends might wind up wishing they had never been rescued.

Over a hundred yards from the Piegan encampment, Nate halted and tied the stallion's reins to a low branch on a spruce tree. "This is where you wait," he announced. "If you hear shooting, head west."

"Which way is that?" Pudge asked, gazing in blatant confusion at the myriad of stars sparkling in the firmament. "How can you tell which way is which once the sun sets?"

"You learn to read the heavens, just like the Indians do," Nate said. He pointed at a group of seven familiar stars that every boy learned about at an early age. "Do you know what that is?"

"Sure. The Big Dipper," Pudge answered.

"Good. Now pretend you draw a line straight out from the two stars that form the bottom of the dipper. Do you see that star all by itself?"

"The real bright one?"

Nate nodded. "That's the North Star. Face it and hold your arms out from your sides. Your left arm will be pointing to the west."

"Amazing," Pudge said, grinning. "I'll never get lost again knowing this."

"Stay alert until I get back," Nate said, and began to walk off.

"Hold it, King," Brian said. "Surely you're not planning to leave us defenseless? Can't you leave at least one of your guns here?"

The request, while reasonable, bothered Nate. His every instinct warned him not to trust the man.

"For Libbie's sake, if for no other reason," Brian added. "What if you're caught? How will we protect her? With our bare hands?"

"I suppose you're right," Nate admitted reluctantly, and stepped over to the blond beauty. "Here. Hold onto this for me," he said, offering the Hawken.

"Are you certain you won't need it?" she asked.

"No. It's best if I have my hands free anyway," Nate said. Hastening into the murky forest, he cautiously skirted the quiet camp until he was hidden in a dense thicket south of the conical forts. A tendril of white smoke wafted upward from the seemingly dead campfire. The slain guard still lay where he had fallen.

All four horses had been secured by lengths of rope to trees flanking the camp. There was abundant grass, and two of the horses were grazing contentedly. The third had lain down, while the fourth was drinking from the creek.

Would they neigh and give him away? Nate wondered, moving from concealment. He stepped lightly to one of the grazing animals, which looked up, chomping noisily, but betrayed no fear. Nor did the second horse he gathered up. The third, the one trying to sleep, snorted and shook its head in annoyance at being disturbed. He patted its neck and scratched behind its ears until it grew calm. Then he unfastened the rope to the fourth horse and led the animals into the trees.

Behind him the Piegans slumbered on.

He was delighted at his success. By first light, when the war party would awaken and find the guard, his little group would be ten miles or better from the creek. Being on foot, the Piegans had no hope of catching them.

Nate reflected on the issue of the two greenhorns in depth. What should he do about the troublemakers? They weren't part of the emigrant train, and it was highly doubtful Simon Banner would want them tagging along. Knowing Banner, Simon might shoot them on sight. But could they be persuaded to head back to the States? He doubted it. Libbie and Brian were in love, and young lovers were notorious for taking rash risks wiser heads would avoid at all costs. Brian had already stolen Libbie from her folks once; there was nothing to stop him from trying again.

It would help immensely if he knew why they had done what they did. Clearly, they had known one another before the Banners left for the promised land. Had Libbie's father forced her to break off with Brian? If so, on what pretext? Did that explain why she hated Simon so much and why she had wanted to die?

There were so many questions and so few answers.

The greenhorns and Libbie were eagerly awaiting him. Brian, he saw, now held the Hawken, and the first thing Nate did upon rejoining them was to walk up and say flatly, "My rifle."

Brian hesitated. "You have two pistols. I'd like to hold onto it for a while."

"My rifle," Nate repeated, extending his right hand, palm up.

"It's only fair that we share your weapons. What if we're attacked? Shouldn't we be able to defend ourselves?"

Nate made no reply. He simply waited, his features flinty, until, with a sigh of displeasure, Brian gave the Hawken to him. Then Nate mounted Pegasus. "I hope all of you can ride bareback," he said.

In a smooth, lithe motion, Libbie vaulted onto one of the other horses and held the rope rein in her left hand. "Don't worry on my account, Mr. King. I was raised on a farm, remember? Before I was seven I could ride like the wind."

Pudge stepped up to an animal and tentatively stroked its mane. "I never have been much of a rider and I've never gone bareback, but I'll do the best I can." Swinging up, he balanced himself and nodded. "All set."

His face a mask of resentment directed at Nate, Brian climbed onto yet a third horse. "I'll hold my own," he declared. "And I'll watch out for Pudge."

"Then let's go," Nate said, taking the lead to the last horse in his left hand. "By nightfall we'll be back at the wagons."

"Do you have any idea what will happen when we get there?" Brian asked testily. "Libbie's father will shoot Pudge and me on sight."

"I won't let him," Nate promised.

"You don't know Simon like we do," Brian said. "He's mean. No, worse than that. He's downright wicked. The man has no consideration for anyone else, and he's not above killing when he feels it's right. The world would be better off without him."

"Those are mighty strong words," Nate remarked, glancing at Libbie in the expectation of her speaking up in her father's behalf. She sat glumly astride her mount, her posture the picture of dejection.

"Every word is true," Brian insisted.

"Maybe," Nate allowed. "But the important thing is that Simon wants his daughter back. And since I agreed to guide the whole family to Fort Hall, I have to see to it that she's returned to her folks no matter what my personal feelings on the matter might be."

"You don't think much of her pa either, do you?"

"I've met nicer people in my time," Nate confessed, and urged Pegasus forward. "Enough jawing for now. This isn't the proper time or place, not when the Piegans might show up at any time."

That got them going, and for the next three hours they rode hard across the benighted landscape, most of the time through thick forest where low limbs and logs posed constant obstacles. When, at length, they entered a wide, grassy valley, Libbie goaded her horse up alongside Nate's.

"Mr. King, I wanted to say that I'm sorry I've put you to so much trouble on my account. But I also want you to know that I would do it again if I had to. Brian and I are going to be married the first chance we get, and I won't let anything stand in our way. Not even my pa."

"I take it you've changed your mind about wanting to die?"

"Brian changed my mind for me. He says we can't allow the past to poison the future. We have to be strong, to do whatever it takes to bring us true happiness." She paused. "There comes a time in a person's life when they have to do what is best for them, not what their parents might think is best for them. Don't misunderstand. We should all honor our fathers and mothers, just as the Good Book tells us to do. But we have to cut the ties if the ties are strangling us." Again she paused. "Does that make sense to you?"

"Perfect sense."

"When I was young I was a dutiful girl. I always did as my folks wanted, and they never had any complaints." Libbie gazed skyward. "I thought they were the most loving, kindest parents a girl could have."

"Something changed your mind?" Nate prompted when she fell silent.

"Yes. I made a mistake. A big mistake, to be honest. But I thought I could count on their love and understanding to help see me through the hard times. I was wrong."

"Is that why you despise your pa so?"

"If you only knew!" Libbie declared, her voice husky with repressed emotion. "He did something so terrible, so disgusting, that I'll bear the scar inside of me for my entire life."

Now was the moment of truth. Nate looked at her, hoping she would finally reveal the key to unraveling the mystery, but Brian came abreast of him on the other side.

"If it bothers you so much to talk about it, dearest, then don't." Brian nodded at Nate. "And there's certainly no need to tell *him* everything. Some secrets are best kept secret."

"I just thought he should know after all we've put him through," Libbie said.

"All he needs to know is that we don't want to go back to your father," Brian said. "How about it, King? What will it take to change your mind?"

"Simon and Alice are counting on me to return her safe and sound," Nate said.

"Even if she doesn't want to be taken to them? Don't her feelings count?"

Nate glanced to the right at the greenhorn, who rode with the makeshift rope rein in his left hand and with his right arm dangling out of sight on the far side. "I have a job to do and I aim to do it."

"What if I paid you to let us go our own way?" Brian proposed. "The savages took all the money I had on me and scattered it on the ground. But I still have several hundred dollars in a bank account. Every penny of it is yours if you'll ride on back to the Banners and tell Simon that you couldn't find us."

"I won't lie. Not for you. Not for anyone."

"What can it hurt? A little white lie?"

"Out here a man is only as good as his word. You might think it strange, but we take great stock in always being honest with folks, in always telling the truth."

Brian studied Nate in the dim light. "Yes, I can see that trying to change your mind is a complete waste of time. I'm sorry, King, that it had to come this. If there was some other way, I'd gladly take it."

"What are you talking about?" Nate asked, and too late saw out of the corner of his eye, Brian's right arm arc up and around, swinging a long, dark object at his head. He tried to raise his arm to block the blow but was unsuccessful. Tremendous pain exploded in his right temple and scores of bright dots appeared before his eyes. Vaguely, he heard a scream. Then a second blow connected and the pain became a tidal wave that swamped his mind and plunged him into abysmal darkness.

Chapter Ten

The sun revived him.

Nate first became aware of the sensation of heat on his face. His cheeks felt warm enough to fry an egg. He also heard the wind shriek past and the rustling of the high grass. Opening his eyes proved a twofold mistake; the bright glare of sunlight hurt them terribly, forcing him to squint, and pounding waves of agony rocked his head. Wincing in torment, he held a hand above his eyes to shield them from the sun and slowly pushed up on one elbow.

He was lying in the middle of the valley, exactly where he had fallen, ringed by an ocean of grass. The position of the sun told him he had been unconscious for seven or eight hours. He touched his temple and felt dried blood.

Rising to his knees, he took stock. The others had taken Pegasus with them. His rifle was gone, as was one of his flintlocks. They had left him a single pistol, but stolen his powder horn and bullet pouch. Thankfully, they had not thought to appropriate his knife or his tomahawk. Close by lay his crumpled, bloodstained beaver hat. Beside it was a broken branch three feet long and as thick as his wrist, also bloodstained.

Nate leaned over to pick up the hat. He had only himself to blame for being left high and dry, since he had failed to keep watch on the others as they negotiated the tracts of woodland during the night. Obviously, Brian had spotted the branch and either hung over the side of his mount to grab it, or else had stopped and taken but fleeting seconds to arm himself. If Nate had stayed more alert, the green-horn wouldn't have been able to take him by surprise.

He placed his hat loosely on his head, and had started to shove to his feet when faintly to his ears came the sound of voices. Indian voices. Twisting, he rose high enough to peer over the top of the grass, and beheld a sight that made his pulse jump.

Just entering the eastern end of the valley was the Piegan war party, strung out in a line in typical fashion, the foremost warrior bent over to better read the sign.

Nate lowered to his hands and knees and scooted to the north, crawling as rapidly as the intense hammering between his ears allowed. He'd figured the Piegans would give up since they had no hope of catching quarry on horseback, but they were a persistent bunch. Perhaps they counted on their former captives stopping to rest. Or the loss of one of their own might have fired them with resolve to seek vengeance.

They were still far off, which gave Nate time to crawl to the closest trees and stand. He knew when they came on the spot where he had fallen they would plainly see what had happened and would realize that one of those they sought was afoot and not much ahead of them.

Turning westward, Nate ran. He gritted his teeth and clenched his fists, resisting the pain as best he was able. To help firm his own resolve he thought of Brian and what he would do to the treacherous vermin when he found him. Because he would find him. No matter how much time was required, nor how far afield he had to range, even back into the States if need be, he would track him down, recover Pegasus and his other possessions, and pay the greenhorn back in kind for the cowardly blow to his head.

At the west end of the valley the trees on the north and south side blended together into a sprawling stretch of pristine forest. Under different circumstances he would have enjoyed the lush scenery. Now he concentrated on making the best time, on avoiding downed trees and thickets that would slow him down.

A flurry of shouts to his rear was evidence the Piegans had found where he had been knocked off his stallion. In a minute they would be after him. Conditioned by the harsh land in which they dwelled, they were as sleek as deer and as muscular as panthers. No white man could hope to match their fleetness unless he was also mountain-bred or as crafty as a fox.

Nate would have to rely on his wits. He covered a quarter of a mile, then saw a mountain on his left. Making toward it, he found a ravine slicing into the underbelly of the mountain and penetrated a hundred yards into it. A 30-foot-high wall on his right, latticed with erosion-worn cracks, afforded the hand-and footholds he needed to climb to the top.

He trotted 50 yards, then angled down the slope and resumed his westward flight. The detour would only slow the Piegans a bit but every bit helped.

All his years in the mountains was paying off in one respect; so far his lungs were holding up remarkably well. Few people in the States were aware of the strain high altitudes put on the human body. Many a trapper, on first venturing into the Rockies, discovered to his chagrin that his body turned traitor. Lungs used to dealing with sea-level altitude had to work much harder a mile or more up, and until a trapper adjusted to the drastic change he had to contend with chronic shortness of breath and difficulty with breathing after strenuous exertion. A few trappers whose bodies were for some unknown reason unable to make the adjustment were compelled to return to the States to sustain their health.

He was doing fine. A mile of steady running had left him only slightly winded. In the forest behind him rose a chorus of excited yips and whoops. The Piegans must be gaining despite his utmost effort.

Casting about for another way to slow them down, Nate spied a cliff composed of solid rock to his right. It was part of a low peak bordering the valley. Sprinting over to the base, he halted and took a few precious seconds to catch his breath. The cliff could be climbed with difficulty, but he had no intention of doing so. Instead, he glanced over his shoulder at the footprints he had made on his approach. He had deliberately slammed his feet down so that each moccasin print was complete and clear.

Now he had to focus every atom of his being on the ruse. Taking a breath, he also took a step backwards, placing his left foot directly down on top of the left footprint he had made just before he stopped. Then he quickly took another step backwards, this time setting his right foot down in the second-to-last track he had made. Ever backwards he went, each stride precise. He must be careful not to smudge the footprints or to leave two impressions. Doing so would be a dead giveaway the Piegans would instantly spot.

Walking backwards, he entered the trees. Next to a cluster of weeds he bunched his leg muscles and jumped, sailing over the weeds and breaking into a sprint the moment his feet touched the ground. How much time had he bought himself? Five minutes? Ten? It all depended on whether the Piegans fell for his ploy and believed he had scaled the cliff.

Not a minute later he heard an uproar when the Piegans came to the base of the rocky height, their impassioned yells echoing hollowly in all directions. They knew they were close behind him, and probably imagined he would soon be in their grasp. Some would climb up, others would flank the cliff on both sides. He heard nothing to indicate that they were aware of his scheme and in hot pursuit.

He allowed himself to relax slightly. His lungs now ached abominably; his arms and legs were becoming sluggish. He had to stop to regain his strength before he was too weak to lift a foot. A stand of aspens afforded the ideal hiding spot, and he moved into the center and knelt.

Nate would have given anything for ten hours of uninterrupted sleep, a luxury he was unlikely to savor for quite some time. He steadied his breathing and leaned against a trunk. As soon as he caught his breath he had to be on his way. To delay was to invite disaster since the Piegans wouldn't stay fooled by his strategy forever.

Fatigue made his limbs feel leaden. He closed his eyes and sagged. His face felt flushed and he was perspiring freely. Mopping his brow, he thought of the scream he had heard when Brian struck him. That must have been Libbie, which meant she had not been expecting the attack. He was glad. He liked her, and he didn't like to think she had been a willing party to such a dastardly act.

Straightening, Nate moved out of the aspens and hiked westward. He figured the others would head in that direction until they came to the Green River Basin. Then they would turn southeast and make for South Pass. His wisest course of action, therefore, might be to return to the emigrants and use one of their horses to catch Libbie and her friends.

Quite by accident he found fresh hoofprints, and recognized those of Pegasus among them. So he was on the right trail. He began trotting, his arms swinging loosely, pacing himself so as not to wear himself out prematurely.

Alternately trotting and briefly resting, he covered another mile. His buckskins were damp with sweat and clung to him like a glove. The sounds of the Piegans had long since faded, and he congratulated himself on outfoxing them.

A green meadow opened out before him. He ran through the tall grass, feeling it swish around his legs. Suddenly a feral shriek cut the air to the rear. Startled, he whirled and nearly tripped over his own feet at the sight of a lone stocky Piegan rushing out of the trees. The warrior waved a war club overhead and increased his speed.

Spinning, Nate ran for all he was worth. Had the Piegans discovered his trick already and were they now all close behind him, or was there only the one man? If he knew the answer to that, he would know whether to use his flintlock or not. The shot was bound to alert the rest, so he didn't want to employ the pistol unless he was positive the entire war party had given chase, in which case it didn't matter if they heard.

Nate decided to save the ball for when he really needed it. He drew his knife on the run and held it close in front of him so the pursuing warrior couldn't see it. He gripped the blade, then intentionally slowed, pretending to be on his last legs, bending over as he glanced over his shoulder to mark the Piegan's advance.

Sensing an easy kill, the warrior was ten yards off and closing like an avenging wraith. His mouth curled in a triumphant grin and he held the war club ready to swing a crushing blow.

Nate slowed to almost a walk. Surreptitiously watching the Piegan, he waited until the man was less than ten feet away before he uncoiled with stunning swiftness and threw the knife. Practice made perfect, as the saying went, and Nate had practiced such a toss on countless occasions.

He'd even won a few knife-and tomahawk-throwing contests at the annual rowdy Rendezvous where the trappers competed in everything from foot races to wrestling to hopping competitions.

The blade caught the Piegan in the chest over the heart and sank in clean to the hilt. He abruptly stopped, dropped his war club, and grabbed the knife. Venting an enraged growl, he tore the blade out, held it in his right hand, and sprang at Nate. But he only took two strides. Then his knees buckled and he sprawled forward to lie still, blood trickling from the corner of his mouth.

Nate knelt to pry his knife from the warrior's fingers. He wiped the blade clean on the grass and stood. In the woods bordering the meadow erupted a series of strident whoops, and he glimpsed painted figures gliding through the trees. So the whole war party was after him! Turning, he slid the knife into its sheath and fled for his life.

Now that the Piegans had him in sight they would run all out; they wouldn't slow down until they overtook him. His main worry was being struck by an arrow. Indian boys were instructed early in the use of the bow, and by the time each boy became a full-fledged warrior he could hit a human-sized target from horseback at a full gallop.

He came to the end of the meadow and plunged into pines. Not a moment too soon. Buzzing like a provoked hornet, a shaft sped out of the blue and thudded into the ground within inches of his left foot. He weaved to the right, then the left, putting as many tree trunks as possible between the Piegans and him.

Unbidden, a terrifying thought entered his mind: He was going to be slain! Outrunning the Piegans was impossible. It was only a matter of time, of mere minutes, before the fastest among them was nipping at his heels.

Frowning, Nate shook his head, dispelling the gloomy notion. Where there was life, there was hope! And so long as he had a single breath remaining in his body he would fight for his survival with all the strength he could muster.

Another arrow clipped a branch to his right. A third streaked over his shoulder and hit a tree.

Nate looked back. Three or four of the Piegans were well ahead of the pack and rapidly narrowing the gap. Of them, two held bows. If only he had his Hawken! But he didn't, and no amount of wishful thinking would change the stark reality of the imminent death confronting him unless he could come up with something fast.

But *what?* What could he possibly do to evade the determined Piegans? All his tricks had failed him and he could think of nothing new.

An arrow snatched at the fringe on his right sleeve. Nate glanced over his shoulder to see one of the bowmen was now 15 yards away and nocking yet another shaft. On impulse he drew the flintlock, halted, and spun. The warrior was raising the bow when the pistol cracked, and the Piegan clutched at his face, then toppled.

The other warriors immediately sought cover.

Nate continued his frantic flight. He would gain a few seconds on them. Perhaps, on second thought, even more. Now that the Piegans knew he had a gun, they would be more cautious and go a trifle slower. Thank goodness they had no way of knowing he was out of ammunition and the flintlock was useless!

He spent over two minutes in running flat out, until his body throbbed with agony and he found the taking of a single breath to be an excruciating ordeal. He was close to the end of his endurance and he knew it. The yips of the pursuing Piegans reminded him they were on the verge of catching him, but there was no reserve of energy for him to draw from that would enable him to pull ahead, nor was there any way of eluding them.

His legs weighed a ton. Despite his wishes, his body slowed of its own accord. His legs refused to cooperate. His lungs screamed in protest. Inhaling raggedly, he stumbled into a clearing and stopped. The least he could do was sell his life dearly. With that in mind he started to draw his tomahawk and butcher knife. Then he froze, wondering if his ears had deceived him.

He'd heard a low whinny.

Looking up, he was stupefied to see a horse walking toward him. And not just any horse; it was Pegasus! The stallion bore dozens of scratch marks on its belly, flanks, and legs, and it was coated thick with sweat.

"I'm seeing things!" Nate blurted. But the apparent apparition came right up to him and touched his neck with its muzzle. He could feel its warm skin, smell its body. "Pegasus?" he said softly, reaching up to touch the stallion's mane.

A cry of baffled rage came from the throat of the first Piegan to spy the animal.

Nate galvanized into motion. Gripping the reins, he swung into the saddle and brought Pegasus around sharply. At a stroke of his legs the stallion plunged into the woods. He hunched low in case one of the warriors tried to bring him down with an arrow, and he hadn't gone five yards when two shafts narrowly missed his head. Then Pegasus reached a gallop and the war party swiftly fell far to the rear.

It had all happened so incredibly fast that Nate feared he was dreaming. Perhaps he had fallen and struck his head and was only imagining the stallion had arrived at the very last instant to pull his hide out of the fire. But the rolling gait of the big horse and the feel of the immensely powerful animal between his legs reassured him that this was real.

Dazed, he rode several miles before he thought to slow down. He was safe. The Piegans could trail him all they wanted, but they'd never catch him now. All thanks to Pegasus.

Leaning forward, he stroked the stallion's neck and spoke soft words of affection. In the past there had been horses he'd liked, some he'd even been quite fond of, but none held a candle to his gift from the Nez Percé.

It was strange. When he'd first received the stallion, the horse had willingly let his wife and son climb on and had taken them for many a pleasant ride. His best friend, Shakespeare McNair, had also ridden Pegasus once. But the more time Nate had spent with the animal, the more it came to regard him as its sole master. Eventually, Pegasus would only let Nate climb up. When others tried, the stallion would snort and kick or rear.

Nate had never known a horse to become so particular, and had mentioned as much to McNair. The aged mountain man had claimed to have known of two or three other horses that had developed exceptional attachments to their owners, and Shakespeare had been of the opinion that it was a blessing in disguise. "No one," Shakespeare had said, "will ever be able to steal this critter. If they try, they'll wind up on their backsides in the dirt."

Was that the explanation for Pegasus turning up at the right place at the right time? Had the stallion broken away from Libbie and the greenhorns and returned to find him? It was the only logical reason that he could see. So Shakespeare, as usual, had been right. Having a superbly devoted animal like Pegasus was a blessing. Never again would he—and he grinned at the thought—look a gift horse in the mouth.

He rode for another hour, until a stream beckoned, then finally halted. Pegasus was parched and gulped the water in great draughts. Sinking to his knees, Nate cupped a mouthful to his dry lips and sipped.

His bedroll and parfleches were still tied to the stallion. Since one of them contained the jerked venison and pemmican Winona had packed, he need not worry about having to waste time hunting game. And since his spare ammunition and black powder were stored in the other, his pistol was no longer useless.

After drinking his fill, Nate attended to the first order of business reloading the flintlock. After the stallion slaked its thirst, he mounted and rode leisurely westward. As much as he wanted to catch up with Brian, he was not going to ride Pegasus into the ground doing it. That Pegasus was weary was self-evident. Nate would have to stop in a while so they both could rest and recuperate.

An hour and a half later he ascended a hill and reined up in a dense group of pines. Confident the stallion would hear or smell anything or anyone that approached, he secured the reins on a tree next to a patch of grass, then crawled under the tree, curled up into a ball, and was immediately asleep.

This time it was a cool breeze from the northwest lightly caressing his face and rattling nearby tree limbs that brought him around. He sat up, rubbed his eyes, and turned.

Pegasus was cropping grass a few feet away.

Crawling out, he straightened, then stretched. His body ached from head to toe, but he was alive and glad to be so. The sun had set hours ago and now a half-moon bathed the countryside in a pale light.

"Ready to travel?" Nate asked, stepping to the stallion, which lifted its head and rubbed against him like an oversized dog. Climbing up, he rode down the hill and bore due west.

Munching on jerky satisfied his hunger. He felt invigorated and raring to tangle with the polecat who had laid him low. Now that he had time to think, he dwelled on the fact his prized Hawken had been stolen, and could barely control his anger. Next to a free trapper's horse, his most important possession was his rifle. Stealing one was a certain death warrant.

Back in '23 a man by the name of Hugh Glass had set the example for all mountaineers. Severely mauled by a she-bear protecting her cubs, he was left to die by the party he was with, abandoned in the most remote region of the mountains without so much as a knife to his name. His associates, certain he would die, took everything he owned but the clothes on his back. Through sheer will-power Hugh Glass survived, and then he commenced an odyssey that became legendary.

Living on berries and the carcasses of game killed by wild beasts, laying low when hostiles came near and avoiding the numerous grizzlies that appeared, Old Glass, as the trappers called him, traveled hundreds and hundreds of miles until he eventually caught up at Henry's Fort with the men who had deserted him. There he learned that one of the party, the man who had taken his rifle, had headed back toward civilization.

Unfazed, Old Glass went on, covering hundreds more miles, going far down the Missouri to near the mouth of the Platte, and there at Fort Atkinson he caught up with the man. Glass would have killed him too, if not for the fact the former trapper had enlisted and wore the uniform of the United States Army. The commanding officer intervened, talking Glass out of seeking revenge, but when Glass cut out for the wilderness again he held his own rifle in his gnarled hands.

Nate could understand Glass's determination. A good rifle often saved a man's hide again and again, so it was only natural for a trapper to come to regard his rifle more as a friend than as merely a lifeless piece of wood and metal. Some mountaineers got into the habit of talking to their rifles like they did to their horses, and no one made light of them for the habit.

Those living in the States seldom understood such a way of life, but to those who experienced the rigors of mountain living such behavior was perfectly all right. And as attached as the whites became to their horses and their guns, they were outdone by the Indians, many of whom would take cherished war ponies into their lodges at night if they feared a raid by an enemy tribe. A prominent Shoshone warrior went so far as to bring his war pony in whenever it rained.

A sharp nicker from Pegasus shattered Nate's idle reverie, and he looked around for the source of the stallion's alarm. He readily found it.

Ten feet off to the left, crouched on a giant log, was an equally giant panther.

Chapter Eleven

Nate instantly reined up and drew the flintlock. He cocked the pistol but held his thumb on the hammer, waiting for the big cat to make the first move. A single shot might not down it, and he didn't want to fire unless he had no choice.

Its pointed ears laid back, its long tail twitching back and forth, the panther uttered a piercing snarl.

Still Nate refused to shoot. He hoped the panther would leave him alone and elect to go seek prey elsewhere. It was rare for the reclusive predators to attack humans, so rare that many Indian tribes regarded panthers as timid. Unlike grizzlies, which would go after any intruders in their domain, more often than not panthers would flee at the first whiff of human scent.

The cat tilted its head, then growled and slowly backed off the log until just its head was visible. In a blur of speed it whirled and vanished in the underbrush.

Nate listened, but heard no sound other than the wind. Not surprising, since few creatures could move more silently than panthers. Carefully lowering the hammer, he tucked the pistol under his wide leather belt and resumed his journey.

Traveling at night was risky business. There were more meat-eaters abroad, heightening the odds of running into one. And a man had to constantly be on the lookout for potential dangers to his mount, such as prairie-dog burrows or other such holes that could cripple a horse in the blink of an eye.

But Nate had no intention of stopping. This was his chance to gain on the greenhorns and Libbie. The trio had not enjoyed a moment of rest since their capture, so they must have been utterly exhausted when they made camp. They'd sleep until dawn, perhaps even later. And he would use those hours to make up the time he had lost.

He thought of Shakespeare's prediction that one day the vast territory west of the Mississippi River would be overrun by men just like Simon Banner and the greenhorns. It was inevitable, Shakespeare had said, because Americans were a restless race who always liked to see what lay over the next horizon. That wanderlust, combined with the need for more and more land as the population grew and grew, would lure countless emigrants westward.

Lord, he prayed McNair was wrong! If emigrants did come by the thousands, it would spell an end to the way of life he knew. The Indians would not stand still for having their land occupied by farmers and ranchers and the like. Warfare would be widespread. And Nate shuddered to think of what would happen to the game now so marvelously abundant. Just as back in the States, the wildlife would be killed off, hunted to near-extinction by those who could see no further ahead than their next meal.

Already beaver were hard to find thanks to the diligent trapping of only several hundred whites. And the mountain buffalo had been drastically thinned out to supply food and blankets for the trappers. The effect of a mass migration would be like that of a plague of locusts, chewing up the land and killing off practically all the wildlife in its path.

Nate gazed fondly out over the sea of trees intermittently eclipsed, as it were, by gigantic islands of stone and dirt, the majestic Rockies that so stirred the souls of those who chose to dwell among them. He never wanted the paradise he had found to change. Should the prediction come true, he would be strongly tempted to join with the Indians in opposing the white onslaught.

Time went by. His thoughts drifted. Toward daylight he reached the basin and turned to the southeast. Searching for tracks could wait until the sun rose. He was positive Libbie and the two men were making for South Pass, so all he had to do was make a beeline for it.

Now he brought Pegasus to a gallop. His eyes roved the region before him seeking a telltale pinpoint of light, although he doubted he would spot one. Any fire left unattended since the evening before would now be extinguished.

A pink and orange tinge graced the eastern skyline when he saw the smoke. Arising from the other side of a hillock a mile away, the gray column signified his hunt was at an end. He slowed to a walk as he neared the base of the small hill and palmed the flintlock.

One of the three must be awake, Nate deduced. Perhaps they had taken turns keeping watch. Reining up, he swung down and moved around the hill until he could see their camp. First he saw the four horses tethered to scrub trees. Then he spied a crude lean-to, the open end facing to the south, away from him. Near it was the fire, beside which squatted Pudge.

Dropping into a crouch, Nate threaded through the grass. He figured Brian and Libbie were still asleep in the lean-to. Well, they were in for a rude awakening! Keeping low, he advanced to within a dozen feet of the fire.

Pudge had the look of someone who was thoroughly miserable. His hair was a mess, he needed a shave, and his homespun clothes were bedraggled. Wedged under his belt was Nate's other pistol. He yawned, then muttered to himself as he warmed his hands.

Nate could see through the gaps between the slender branches forming the wall of the lean-to. Glimpses of golden tresses told him Libbie was lying nearest the back, so Brian must be at the front. Stealthily rising and tiptoeing forward, he came up behind Pudge and lightly touched his flintlock to the greenhorn's head. "Don't make a sound," he warned.

Gasping in fright, Pudge went rigid.

"Did you really think I wouldn't find you?" Nate asked softly, and leaned forward to grab the stolen pistol. Then he moved around to where Pudge could see him. The greenhorn swallowed and looked as if he wanted to dig a hole to hide in. "Give me one good reason why I shouldn't shoot you here and now," Nate said.

"Please, Mr. King," Pudge blubbered. "It wasn't my idea to knock you out and steal your things. Brian did it all on his own. I'm sorry it happened. I truly am."

"Not as sorry as you're going to be. I'm of half a mind to take Libbie on back to her folks and leave the two of you here afoot."

"You wouldn't!"

Nate glanced at the lean-to and raised his voice. "All right, you two! Rise and shine! Company has come calling." He trained both pistols in their direction. "And I want your hands where I can see them or one of you might end up eating lead for breakfast."

He saw Libbie sit up, and grinned at the shock both she and Brian must be experiencing. A moment later she stepped into the open, smoothing her dress down and gazing in amazement at him.

"Mr. King! You're all right! Thank God!"

"As well as a horse like few others," Nate added, wagging a pistol to beckon her closer. He stared at the lean-to, eagerly waiting for her beau to emerge. The prospect of paying Brian back made him tingle with anticipation.

"I'm so glad you weren't hurt," Libbie said sincerely. "I was totally against what Brian did to you, and I tried to get him to revive you and bring you along but he refused to listen."

Nate was wondering why the bastard had yet to appear. He peered at the wall of the lean-to but saw no one moving within. "Where is the no-account varmint?"

"Right behind you!" snapped the gleeful voice of the other greenhorn. "And I've got your rifle pointed at your spine. So if you know what's good for you, you'll drop those pistols and turn around."

For a few seconds Nate hesitated. His reflexes being what they were, he was confident he could step to one side, spin, and fire before Brian got off a shot. Then he heard the distinct click of the Hawken's hammer being cocked. Unfortunately, Libbie was in front of him. If Brian did manage to fire, or simply squeezed the trigger as he fell, the ball might accidentally strike her. Or possibly Pudge if the shot went wild. And he had no grudge against either of them.

"I'm waiting, King," Brian said. "I don't want to shoot you if I can avoid it, but I'll be damned if I'm letting you take Libbie back to her pa. Now put down those pistols!"

Reluctantly, his every instinct telling him he was making a great mistake, Nate lowered the flintlocks to the earth and released them. As he straightened, Brian laughed.

"You mountain men aren't as tough as you're made out to be. We hear all these fantastic stories about how your kind can lick dozens of Injuns with their bare hands and kill grizzlies with just their knives, but it's all hogwash. This is twice I've gotten the better of you."

"Don't remind me," Nate said, his temper soaring. Pivoting, he stared down the barrel of his rifle.

Brian beamed and nodded at the hill to his rear. "I was up yonder keeping watch when you showed up. In another five minutes Pudge would have relieved me." Giving Nate a wide berth, he walked to Libbie's side. "You're too persistent for your own good, Mr. King. What am I going to do with you?"

"I won't have you hurting him again," Libbie declared. "You never should have struck him in the first place."

"What choice did he leave me?" Brian countered. "You were there. I tried to talk him out of taking you back but he wouldn't listen. I even offered him every dollar I have, yet he refused to accept it." Brian scowled. "I didn't like taking unfair advantage of him anymore than you did, my love. Can I help it if he's too thickheaded for his own good?"

Pudge stood and joined them. "What are we going to do with him, Brian?"

"We let him go," Libbie said quickly.

"That would be dumb," Brian declared. "He'd only follow us until he found some way to take us by surprise, then he'd force you to go with him. Is that what you want?"

"No," Libbie answered.

"How about if we take his horse and leave him here?" Pudge suggested. "He'd never catch us."

"That's what we figured before," Brian said, "but that pied nightmare of his tore loose and took off on its own." He glared at Nate. "Your stallion about caved in my head. We'd stopped for a short rest and I was leading it to water when it tore the reins from my hands and ran away. I tried to stop it but it reared on me and knocked me down."

"Pegasus knows a polecat when he sees one."

"Funny man," Brian barked, and nudged Pudge with his elbow. "Get something to tie him with and do it as tight as you can. I don't want him giving us any more trouble."

While he was covered by the Hawken, there was nothing Nate could do as Pudge took a lead rope off of one of the horses and came over to bind him. Pudge used Nate's knife to cut off a piece.

"Sorry again, Mr. King," the hefty youth apologized, then pulled Nate's arms behind his back, looped the rope about Nate's wrists, and secured it with three knots. "There. All done."

Smiling smugly, Brian lowered the Hawken and let the hammer down. "Have a seat, King," he said in a mocking tone, and gestured at a spot near the fire. "I'd offer you some coffee, but I'm afraid we don't have any since you wouldn't try to reclaim our supplies from those savages."

"Don't treat him so, Brian," Libbie scolded.

Nate eased to the ground and crossed his legs. Once again he had taken the greenhorns too lightly and paid for his folly. Once he got free, he would not make the same error in judgment a third time. Glumly, he stared into the crackling flames and resigned himself to being their prisoner for a while.

"Pudge, go try and catch his stallion," Brian directed. "It's grazing on the other side of the hill."

"Why me?" Pudge responded.

"Because I'm not letting Libbie out of my sight," Brian said, sitting across from Nate. "Take the two flintlocks if it will make you feel any better."

"You bet it will," Pudge stated, gladly scooping up both guns. He took a few strides, then paused, fingering the weapons and gazing anxiously out over the open land to the south and west. "What if there are Injuns watching us?"

"I doubt it, or Mr. King wouldn't have walked into our camp the way he did," Brian said. "We're safe. Don't worry."

"Are you in your right mind? I won't stop worrying until we're safe at Fort Leavenworth," Pudge asserted. Bracing his round shoulders, he tramped off to do Brian's bidding.

"Do you really believe you'll make it all the way to Fort Leavenworth with no food and no water?" Nate casually asked. "A person can die of thirst and hunger on the prairie just as easily as from a hostile's arrow or lance."

"Not if that person knows where to find water and game," Brian said.

"And you do?"

"No. You do."

Libbie looked from one to the other. "What are you getting at, dearest?"

"Simply this. Mr. King here must know the Plains as well as he does the mountains. If we take him with us, he'll have to lead us to water and game if he doesn't want to die along the way. So I propose we make him our unwilling companion until we reach civilization."

"And what then?" Libbie inquired.

"Why, we let him go, of course. What can he do then? We'll explain everything to the officer in charge at Leavenworth and I'm sure he'll see things our way. And since the Army has no jurisdiction out here, King can't press charges." He chuckled. "Have no fear. Once we're at the fort, we'll be safe. The Army isn't about to let him murder any of us."

"But it's not right to drag him across the prairie against his will."

"Then give me a better idea," Brian said.

Libbie opened her mouth, closed it, opened it again. "I don't have one," she confessed.

"I do," Nate addressed Brian. "Allow me to take Libbie

to her folks. Pudge and you can ride along and I'll convince Simon to let the two of you join us."

"We've discussed that before and I told you what would happen," Brian said. "No thank you, mountain man. My way is the best."

Further argument would be useless, Nate realized. The younger man had his mind made up, and that was all there was to it. Nate had to exercise the patience of a Shoshone warrior until his chance to turn the tables came, and come it would. Traversing the prairie would take weeks. During one of the times when Brian slept, Nate would teach the arrogant greenhorn just how resourceful mountain men could be.

"Mr. King," Libbie said, "it would have been best for everyone if you had gone back to my folks instead of coming after us. Why didn't you leave well enough alone?"

"And let your true love get the best of me?"

"I see. Your pride was wounded."

"No, my head," Nate corrected her. "You don't see at all, Libbie, because you were born and bred in the States. You don't know that out here a man is measured differently than he is back there. In the States a man is a success if he has a lot of money and power." Nate noticed Brian yawning. "Out here a man is measured several ways, and one of the most important is the measure of his courage. The indians count coup to settle who is the bravest. For free trappers like myself, our reputations take the place of counting coup, although quite a few of us do that at times."

"*You've* counted coup?" she said in surprise.

"Many times," Nate admitted. "I'm an adopted member of the Shoshone tribe. If I didn't count coup, I wouldn't be considered a warrior. I wouldn't be allowed to sit in the councils with the men."

Brian threw back his head and cackled, then glanced at Libbie. "Don't this beat all! Your precious mountain man is as much a savage as those red devils who took us captive."

"It's not like that at all," Nate said harshly. "It's more like earning rank in the army. An Indian starts by going out and stealing a few horses or killing an enemy or two, and in so doing he qualifies to be a warrior. He continues to advance in standing in his tribe by adding to the brave deeds he's done. Eventually he works his way up to become what you might call a Little Chief. And after stealing a certain high number of horses and taking a lot of scalps, he may even earn the title of Great Chief."

"How quaint," Brian commented.

Nate would have slugged the man if his hands were free. Since he had Libbie's thoughtful attention, he went on. "Becoming a warrior is the most important goal in a young Indian's life. If he hasn't done any brave deeds by the time he's twenty, then he's not allowed to take part in councils and has to do the same work as the women. In some tribes the women even get to order him around. No man wants to suffer such a fate." He paused. "So Indians don't count coup just to see who can be the most savage. They do it as a measure of their manhood."

"I think I understand," she said.

"Who cares what Indians do?" Brian interjected. "They all deserve to be rounded up just like cattle and put wherever the government wants to put them. That's what President Jackson said and I believe him."

"You would," Nate muttered.

Brian bristled and started to lift the Hawken; then his gaze went past Nate and he stood. "Where's the stallion?"

"I couldn't get close," Pudge announced. "It saw me coming around the hill and took off like a bat out of hell. Chasing it would have been a waste of time." Walking up beside Nate, he looked down and grinned. "That's sure some horse you've got there, Mr. King."

"Believe me, I know."

"Enough talk," Brian said curtly. "Let's mount and head for South Pass. I know we're all hungry and we haven't eaten since we left the Piegan camp, but by nightfall, with some luck, I'll bag something to eat."

"I hope so," Pudge said. "At this rate, when we get back home folks will change my nickname to Skinny."

It was Pudge who helped Nate get on one of their horses. Brian put out the fire. Libbie went into the lean-to and did whatever women do so that when she came back out she was as radiant as sunshine and her clothes were hardly ruffled at all. And she did it all without a drop of water or the use of comb and brush.

Brian assumed the lead, Libbie riding by his side. Pudge had to lead the animal bearing Nate. They bore to the southeast, holding their horses to a trot that rapidly ate up the miles. Several times Pudge looked at Nate and seemed about to speak, but he always glanced away moments later without saying what was on his mind.

Over an hour after leaving camp, Pudge looked at Nate yet one more time, then suddenly looked startled and pointed to their rear. "I'll be damned! Take a gander at that!"

Twisting, Nate saw Pegasus five hundred yards off, following them. The stallion was cleverly matching their gait and speed. By staying that far out, it could easily avoid being caught should Brian or Pudge go after it. Nate grinned and wished he had the stallion under him instead of the bay he was on.

"What the hell!" Brian declared, having looked over his shoulder at the yell from Pudge. Reining up, he turned his horse and glared at Pegasus. "It's that contrary cuss again! For two cents I'd blow its brains all over the prairie." He raised the Hawken and sighted down the barrel.

By then Nate was almost abreast of Brian's mount since Pudge had not yet stopped. He didn't know whether Brian would really fire, and although the range was too great for any degree of accuracy, he wasn't going to risk his stallion being struck through sheer dumb luck. So as he came even with Brian's mount, he leaned to the side and used his legs to propel himself like a human battering ram at the greenhorn.

Engrossed in taking a bead, Brian was caught off-guard. Nate's head slammed into his side, throwing him off balance, and together they toppled from his horse onto the grass.

Nate landed on his left side and rolled. He heard Brian curse, then surged upright, applying his shoulder against the ground for leverage. As he straightened he lashed out with his right foot, catching the sluggish greenhorn in the pit of the stomach. Brian doubled over, sputtering and wheezing, and Nate followed through with a second kick to the tip of Brian's chin that stretched the younger man out like a board.

"Mr. King, don't!" Libbie wailed. She had drawn rein ten yards ahead, but now she goaded her horse toward them.

Nate quickly sat down, tucked his knees to his chest, and straining mightily, worked his bound hands up over the back of his legs until they cleared his feet. Close by lay his Hawken. Although his wrists were tied, his fingers were loose enough to permit him to grab the rifle and point it at Brian.

"No!" Libbie cried, stopping mere feet away.

Disregarding her, Nate managed to cock the Hawken and touched a finger to the trigger. He was forced to hold the gun awkwardly, but there was no doubt in anyone's mind that he could fire if he was so inclined.

Blinking several times, Brian groaned and rose on his elbows. "You bastard," he said, blood trickling from the corner of his mouth. "You almost broke my jaw."

"I tried my best," Nate countered, backing up to give himself room to maneuver should one of them come at him. That was when he noticed Pudge. The hefty green-horn had swung around but had not drawn a flintlock. Instead, Pudge was staring to the southwest, his forehead knit in perplexity. Overcome by curiosity, Nate shifted in the same direction and felt the short hairs at the base of his neck prickle. A mile off was a long brown line resembling for all the world a brown wave rolling across the basin.

"What the dickens am I looking at?" Pudge asked.

"It's a buffalo stampede," Nate answered, "and they're heading right this way."

Chapter Twelve

"Dear God!" Pudge blurted out in horror.

"What do we do?" Libbie asked.

"We get out of their path or we get trampled," Nate said, and stepped up to her horse. "I need your help. Climb down and cut me loose. And hurry."

"No!" Brian roared, pushing off the ground and taking an unsteady stride, his fists balled at his waist. "Don't you dare listen to him, Libbie!"

Pivoting, Nate leveled the Hawken. "Not another step, polecat," he warned, "or I'll put a ball through you." His steely tone stopped Brian cold. The greenhorn made no response, his eyes pools of simmering hatred.

Suddenly they all heard the sound of distant drumming, like thunder rumbling far off.

"You'd better hurry," Nate reminded Libbie.

She needed no further persuasion. Jumping down, she used his own butcher knife to slice through the ropes, and tossed them at his feet when she was done. "Which way do we go?" she then asked apprehensively.

The same question was uppermost in Nate's mind. The buffalo were spread out over a half-mile front and were now only three quarters of a mile off. It was a small herd, but trying to outflank it would be a risky proposition. If one of their horses flagged, its rider was doomed.

When buffaloes stampeded, they stopped for nothing. Nothing at all. Which was why Indians often surrounded a herd, provoked a stampede in the direction of a convenient cliff, and drove hundreds of the dumb brutes to their deaths. Afterward, there was always plenty of meat for everyone in the village and much rejoicing.

"What got them going?" Pudge wondered.

"Anything under the sun," Nate said, about to issue instructions when he remembered something he had to do. Hastening over to Pudge's horse, he extended his right hand. "Both of my pistols. Now."

"Yes, sir. Whatever you say," Pudge said, transparently glad to comply. "Just save us from those monsters, will you?"

Nate pointed to the northwest, at part of the range of hills and mountains forming the eastern boundary of the Green River Basin. The nearest foothill stood less than a mile off. "Ride for your lives," he advised. "When you reach the trees, don't stop. Make for high ground and the herd should pass you by."

"Should?" Libbie said.

Pudge wasted no words. His legs flapping against his mount, he slanted toward the closest foothill, dust rising in large puffs from under the flying hoofs of his animal.

"You too," Nate said, running up behind Libbie's horse and giving it a smack on the rump. In a flash she was racing after Pudge.

"What about me?" Brian asked. "I suppose you'll take the other two horses and leave me here to be crushed to a pulp."

"You take them."

"What?" Brian said, as if unsure he had heard correctly.

"You take them," Nate repeated, and sprinted madly toward Pegasus. The stallion had halted four hundred yards away and was staring intently at the swelling line of onrushing bison. "Pegasus!" Nate shouted, waving his arms. "Come to me! Come on!"

If the stallion recognized him, it made no move to obey. Perhaps fascinated by the fury of the stampede, it simply stood there and stared.

"Pegasus! Don't just stand there, you simpleton!" Nate bellowed, his limbs flying, running as he had seldom run before. Pegasus looked at him but didn't move. Of all the times for the stallion to be fickle! "Come on, darn you!" he yelled. "Or we're both goners!"

At last Pegasus moved to intercept him, but at a walk, not a trot.

"Faster, damn you!" Nate urged. Well past the stallion he could see the front ranks of buffaloes, their shaggy heads low to the ground, their massive bodies partially obscured by the thick dust cloud swirling from underneath them. Was there time for him to mount and reach the hills before the herd did? It would be close. Too close.

Pegasus moved faster, reaching a trot in seconds.

When the stallion was almost upon him, Nate swerved two steps to the right, let the big horse come alongside, and vaulted into the saddle while Pegasus was still in motion. The Hawken clutched tight in his left hand, he worked the reins and his legs and was immediately speeding for the sanctuary of the inviting green hills.

Pudge was hundreds of yards ahead. Libbie rode close in his wake. Brian, astride their third horse, was halfway between Nate and the others. The last horse, the bay, had been left exactly where it had stopped after Nate jumped off it. He glanced at the abandoned animal but did not veer from his course; any further delay would prove too costly. The bay would have to fend for itself.

The thundering of the herd grew and grew, until looking back Nate could see the wicked, curved horns of the leaders and imagined he could also see their brooding dark eyes and their flaring nostrils. Pegasus was galloping as fast as Pegasus could go and still the herd appeared to be gaining. Nate bent forward, his heart beating wildly in time to the driving rhythm of the stallion's hoofs. *Go! Go! Go!* he shrieked in his mind.

Repeatedly he glanced at the buffaloes, fearful he had gotten underway too late. On his next glance he saw the bay break into a run. Belatedly, it had realized the urgency of fleeing. That most basic of creature instincts, self-preservation, sparked the bay into a mad dash for its life, a dash that it lost not a minute later.

The first squeal was almost humanlike, so much so that it chilled Nate's skin. He saw the front rank of bison overhaul the terrified horse, saw the bay go down amid a swirl of hoofs and tails and slashing horns. Some of the foremost buffaloes tried to jump over the obstacle, and failed. Those behind the leaders never wavered, never parted even slightly. Their hoofs reduced the bay to a pulpy mass in the time it would take a man to pull on his boots.

Nate graphically knew what to expect should he suffer the same horrendous fate. Like the wind he rode, and like a raging storm the stampeding herd pursued him. He set his eyes on the first hill to the exclusion of all else. If he went down, it wouldn't be for a lack of trying.

Each second became an eternity. The buffaloes didn't gain any more ground, nor did they lose any.

Pudge was the first among the trees, and as Nate had directed he headed straight for the crown of the hill. Seconds later Libbie did likewise.

Nate had given that advice because he had witnessed stampedes before, and knew from prior observation that herds invariably broke in half at the base of hills and mountains to sweep around on either side rather than go up and over the crest. He counted on these buffaloes doing the same.

But could he reach the top before them? Despite the stallion's superb performance, the bison would be so close at the bottom of the hill that if the stallion stumbled just once on the slope the herd would be on them before Pegasus recovered. So Nate opted to change his tactic.

Presently the hill loomed before him. With a jerk of the reins he cut sharply to the left, hugging the bottom. To his rear a tremendous din of earth-shaking proportions drowned out all other sound. The ground itself seemed to tremble. He glanced upward and glimpsed Brian racing up the slope. Libbie and Pudge were lost among the trees, and he hoped they would reach the top safely.

He dared to look at the herd just as the seething mass of unstoppable brutes reached the hill. As he had expected, the buffaloes parted, some bearing right, some left. But, to his consternation, not all imitated the example of those in the foremost ranks. A large bunch in the middle of the mass went straight up the hill, straight toward Libbie and the greenhorns!

His hope of evading the herd was now diminished. He'd intended to go around to the far side, then angle up the slope. But if he did so now, he'd run smack-dab into the portion of the herd going up and over. So he must come up with another brainstorm, and do it quickly.

Pegasus flew to the opposite side. Already a few buffaloes had appeared at the south end. Instantly Nate cut to the left, bearing due east, barreling into pines and brush that crackled as he plowed through.

The two prongs of the herd were sweeping around the hill as the third bunch rumbled over the top.

Faintly, Nate heard a scream. Or was it his imagination? He tried not to think of what might have happened to

Libbie if she had been caught in the open. He couldn't do her any good anyway, not unless and until he saved his own skin.

The swiftest buffaloes were not more than 30 yards behind him. They charged into the forest with the force of a tornado, smashing aside anything and everything in their way.

Nate weaved among trunks and hurdled logs while casting about for a means of escape. He anticipated the stampede would lose its momentum before too long. The trick was to stay alive till then. Bearing to the left, he sought for the end of the foremost line of bison, but saw only beast after beast after beast.

On and on he rode, losing sight of the hill because of the canopy of limbs overhead. Without warning the trees thinned and he found himself in a narrow valley. Heading up the center, the wind rushing past his face, he searched for a way out of his predicament. *Any* way out would do. He wasn't fussy.

The valley bore to the right, meandering between a pair of jagged peaks, one of which threw an enormous shadow across the valley floor.

"Yea, though I walk through the valley of the shadow of death," Nate thought to himself, and suddenly stiffened on seeing that which promised to make the quotation come true. Two hundred yards ahead reared a rugged bluff. The valley was a trap!

To the right and left were steep slopes, so steep Pegasus would not be able to climb either without falling. To his rear arose the constant rolling thunder of the herd. A hasty glance showed him the buffaloes had him completely boxed in.

Of all the rotten times for his luck to run out! Nate reflected, desperately scanning the slopes and the bluff. He was not at all ready to meet his Maker; he had a wife and son depending on him for their sustenance. And of all the ways to be killed, being caught in a stampede had to be one of his least favorite. It would be much better to die in bed wearing a smile on his lips, and nothing else.

He was almost to the bluff. The bison had slowed, but not enough. They promised to sweep right up to the bottom of the bluff, and in the process to bury him beneath tons upon tons of hurtling sinew and muscle.

Then Nate spotted the game trail where the bluff and the slope on the right blended together. It wasn't much of one, a winding ribbon stretching from the valley floor to near the top of the peak, but he was in no mood to quibble. As the old saying stated so well, beggars couldn't be choosers. Either he took the trail or he died.

Incentive like that took him up the slope faster than was prudent. Pegasus slipped, faltered, and was on the verge of falling when Nate hauled on the reins and shifted his balance, giving the stallion help enough to carry it forward. From there on up he was compelled to take the ascent slowly, his gaze riveted on the herd below.

The buffaloes were moving at a trifle of their previous speed when the leaders came to the bluff and halted. Those pressing so tightly together in the main body of the herd did the same, and within moments what had once been a panicked horde of bison resembled more a peacefully grazing herd of tame cattle.

Nate climbed steadily. The only tracks on the game trail were those of bighorn sheep, and he marveled that the big stallion could negotiate the same terrain. Toward the top the going became exceedingly difficult. Pegasus slipped time and again, but never fell.

"You can do it, boy," Nate coaxed, and wasn't disappointed. Not quite an hour after commencing the ascent, they came to where the trail led over the crest and down into another valley. Pausing, he surveyed the tranquil herd, then gazed to the west at the distant hill where he had last seen the greenhorns and Libbie. Were any of them still alive?

The descent took half the time of the climb. Once at the bottom of the spacious valley, he turned toward the hill. He felt weary and slumped in the saddle. Having pushed Pegasus so hard in fleeing from the buffaloes, he let the horse take its sweet time, although he was sorely tempted to gallop the entire way.

The countryside lay entombed in silence when he arrived. None of the usual wildlife was present, every animal that could having fled at the onset of the onrushing herd. Eventually the birds and squirrels would come out of hiding and the forest would resume its normal pattern of life, but for the time being it was as if he rode across an alien landscape devoid of life.

"Libbie?" Nate called out at the base of the hill. "Are you up there?"

The only answer was the sighing wind.

Most of the hill was a shambles. From top to bottom the buffaloes had flattened the underbrush, uprooted and flattened trees, and scarred the earth with their iron hoofs.

Nate rode upward, scouring for sign. At the top he halted. The west slope was in the same condition as the east. Broken limbs lay everywhere. Bent and snapped trees made a mockery of Nature's design. "Libbie?" he repeated, to no avail. He started down slowly, his eyes roaming over the blistered slope, then reined up on spying a large lump of bloody flesh off to the left.

The general outline baffled him until he detected the wispy vestige of a tail and realized he was staring at the hindquarters of one of the horses. The animal had been literally torn apart. Moving closer, he saw a torn leg, then another, both ruptured, the cracked bones exposed. Scattered bits of grass, pine needles, and clods of dirt partially covered the horse's head, but not enough to conceal the pulverized flesh and the bulging eyes.

Nate had seldom seen such a revolting sight, and his stomach churned. The implications were even more upsetting. If a horse had gone down, so had its rider. So which one had paid the ultimate price for foolishly trying to grapple with the wilderness on its own terms when all three of them were woefully ignorant of the basics of wilderness survival? Which one would have been better off staying in the States, where the worst a man had to contend with was an occasional marauding black bear or a poisonous snake?

He saw a leg jutting from out of a smashed thicket and at first mistook it for part of a tree trunk. Then he saw the shoe and the homespun pants, both coated with dried blood. Inwardly, he was relieved. The horse had not been Libbie's. "Please let it be Brian," he said to himself, stopping beside the mangled mess lying in the midst of shattered limbs and crushed leaves. "Please."

But it wasn't.

Pudge had fallen onto his back and had never had the chance to rise. Hundreds of driving hoofs had reduced his body to the consistency of pudding. Strangely enough, except for a pair of slash marks on his right cheek and a lot of grime, his face was intact. His eyes were wide open, his mouth the same, his tongue poking out. He had screamed as death claimed him, but it was doubtful he had heard it over the din of the herd.

Nate climbed down and gathered up enough branches and brush to cover the greenhorn's head. It was the least he could do. No, not quite, he promptly corrected himself. There was one more thing. Pudge deserved to go properly.

He stood for a moment with bowed head, trying to think of the right words to say, but except for a passable knowledge of the Psalms and the words of Jesus, he wasn't much good at quoting from the Bible. Feeling uncomfortable, he tried anyway.

"Forgive him, Lord, for being a dunderhead. He had no business being out here. But he came because his friend did, and, if I recollect rightly, 'Greater love hath no man than this, that a man lay down his life for his friends.' If that's the case, then Pudge here died the way a man should, and I hope his soul makes it to your side. Amen."

Mounting, he grimly resumed his search. The others must have suffered a similar grisly fate. He dreaded finding Libbie, but he wouldn't stop until he did. She also deserved to have a few words spoken over her remains. He would leave Brian for the vultures and the coyotes.

An hour of intensive hunting, crisscrossing the slope again and again, produced no results. He stopped at the bottom and scratched his chin. If Libbie and Brian had been trampled, he should have found some trace. Since he hadn't, both must have somehow survived. Then where had they gone?

The obvious answer drew his gaze to the southeast. "Damn, not again," he muttered, and broke into a gallop. The pair had a two-hour head start. If he overtook them by noon he would be fortunate.

Once Nate rode clear of the ground torn up by the bison, he immediately spied two sets of fresh horse tracks leading in the general direction of South Pass. Brian had wasted no time. Nate figured they had cut out the minute the buffalo had passed over the hill. Or the minute after they'd found poor Pudge.

A rare, cold hatred seeped into Nate's soul. He imagined what it would be like to seize Brian in his hands and throttle the life from the bastard. The greenhorn had been an unending source of trouble ever since they met. And now, once again, Brian was bucking the wishes of Libbie's parents and trying to get her out of the territory at all costs. The idiot! Didn't he realize the pair of them stood little chance of crossing the prairie alone and unarmed?

He wondered what she saw in the man. Brian was handsome, he supposed, but a flashing smile wasn't everything. Inner qualities counted for more, qualities like courage and devotion and loyalty. And a dash of common sense, which Brian evidently lacked.

This time he would not go easy on them. He would truss Libbie up, if need be, and throw her on her horse. If Brian objected—and Nate hoped he did—then Nate would thrash Brian within an inch of his life. Possibly closer. Libbie must cease acting like a child and do what was best for the Banner family.

The hours elapsed slowly. From the depth and spacing of the tracks, Nate gathered that Libbie and the greenhorn were riding their animals into the ground. They had yet to learn that he would catch them no matter how fast or how far they rode.

Noon came and went.

Since his throat was parched, he knew Pegasus was equally thirsty. So when he came abreast of a hill known to have a year-round spring on its north side, he strayed from the trail to give them both a short rest. The ice-cold water was delicious and he drank to his heart's content. Pegasus was still drinking when he leaned against a boulder and rested the Hawken in his lap.

He thought of the Banners and the Websters, who must be besides themselves by now over his prolonged absence. Were they waiting for him to return, or in their impatience had they continued westward? If so, they might well be dead, meaning all his hard effort was being wasted. Time would tell.

Given the ability demonstrated by the emigrants, Nate sincerely hoped that great numbers of them would *not* flock to the promised land, for their own sakes. Many, far too many, would perish before they ever saw the crashing surf of the Pacific Ocean. And a line of bleached bones would be the only legacy they left behind.

Or would it?

Nate remembered all the quaint if sparse settlements along the frontier where hard-working men and women eked out spartan existences by wrestling day in and day out with a harsh land that fought them every step of the way. Drought, insects, hostiles, floods; all these the hardy breed of settlers took in stride, refusing to give up in the face of cruel adversity.

Perhaps he had misjudged them. He still didn't want thousands of greenhorns to invade the Indian lands, but he now knew that if they did, they would come to stay. The Indians would be unable to drive them off, and in the long run the prairie and the mountains would become just another stepping-stone on the path to American's conquest of the continent.

A buzzing bee intruded on his reflection and he stood. What had gotten into him? It didn't do for a man to ponder weighty matters when he should be tending to business. Pegasus was done, so he climbed up and headed out, bearing, as ever, to the southeast.

When the dots appeared, Nate didn't quite know what to make of them. There were two, on the horizon, not moving at all. Whatever they were, they must be big. He doubted they were buffalo or elk, which left a single, troubling, likelihood.

Riding closer, he distinguished the silhouettes of a pair of horses. That spurred him to ride at a gallop until he was within 50 yards of the pair; then he slowed. They were the horses Libbie and Brian had been riding, but there was no trace of the lovely girl or her beau.

Puzzled, suspecting the handiwork of hostiles, Nate cocked the Hawken and rode to within 20 feet, then drew rein. Sliding down, he warily advanced. The horses simply gazed at him. He saw that the high grass all around them had been trampled down but bore no evidence of hoof marks. Something other than the horses must have been responsible. Glancing to the right and left, concerned he was blundering into a trap, he strode toward the animal Libbie had been riding. He had a yard to cover when suddenly something grabbed hold of both his ankles and he was brutally slammed to the earth.

Chapter Thirteen

Nate had to let go of the Hawken and throw out his hands to cushion the impact. The pressure on his ankles relaxed, but was instantly replaced by something encircling his knees, and looking down he saw that Brian had seized hold of him and was trying to keep him pinned to the ground. He also saw how he had been tricked. There was a shallow depression, not more than a foot deep but at least 12 feet long, that the devious greenhorn and Libbie had used as their hiding place; they had lain down in it earlier and then covered themselves with flattened grass. If he had been more attentive, he might have figured out their ploy. Nate wanted to kick himself. He had stupidly walked right into their trap, and they had him right where they wanted him.

Now Libbie was also emerging from concealment, her fair features etched with the same somber desperation as Brian's. "Get his pistols!" Brian screeched.

Shocked to find Libbie working in concert with the greenhorn, Nate belatedly made a grab for his right flintlock. But Libbie reached him before his hand could close on the gun and grabbed his wrist.

"Please, Mr. King!" she cried. "Don't resist and we won't hurt you!"

Nate could feel Brian clawing higher, toward his waist, and he streaked his left hand down, grasping the other pistol. Again, though, Libbie thwarted him by grabbing his wrist.

"Please!" she pleaded.

Thinking only of what would happen should Brian gain possession of one of his weapons, Nate wrenched his arms up and out, tearing loose from Libbie, and threw himself to the left, away from her, trying to roll but unable to do more than twist because of Brian's hold on his legs. He kicked out, or attempted to, his leverage limited by the weight of the greenhorn's body.

Libbie lunged at his knife.

Nate shoved her aside and she tripped and fell. Bending forward, he delivered a punch to the side of Brian's head. The greenhorn abruptly let go of his legs, surging upward and snatching at one of the flintlocks. Nate pounded him again. Suddenly Brian vented an inarticulate snarl of rage, dived at his throat, and wrapped both hands around his neck.

Together they rolled over and over. Locked face-to-face, they fought as men driven.

Nate felt Brian's fingers gouging into his windpipe, cutting off his air, and he whipped a right that cracked hard on the greenhorn's chin. But Brian clung fast. Another blow rocked him and his grip slackened slightly.

"Stop it, please!" Libbie wailed.

Neither man heeded her. Brian, beet red, his veins bulging, was trying with all his might to throttle the life from Nate. For his part, Nate gasped for air and struggled to pry Brian's steely fingers off his neck. He was amazed at the man's strength. It was as if Brian had inexplicably become as strong as ten men.

Nate hurled himself to the left, then immediately reversed direction in an effort to throw Brian off balance. He was only partially successful. Brian's body slipped to one side, but the man's fingers remained locked on his throat. Already Nate's lungs were burning in anguish. He began to feel light-headed and knew he must get air to them and get air to them *now*.

If there was one lesson Nate had learned from his Shoshone friends about mortal combat, that lesson could be summed up in two words. Anything goes. When a warrior's life was on the line, he did whatever it took to prevail. Biting, scratching, kicking, they were all done in the heat of intense battle when the difference between time and eternity hung in the balance. So it was that Nate entertained no compunctions about snapping both hands up and gouging his thumbs into Brian's eyes, digging his nails in as far as he could.

The greenhorn yelped and released his hold as he tried to protect his precious sight.

At the very moment that Brian's hands fell from Nate's neck, Nate rolled yet again, to one knee, and rammed his right fist into the greenhorn's face. Brian toppled, groaning and sputtering, his hands pressed to his eyelids.

"You've blinded me! You've blinded me!"

Taking deep breaths, Nate shoved upright and drew his flintlocks. "I doubt it," he muttered. "Now on your feet." He took a step and prodded Brian with his toe.

"I can't see, I tell you!"

Libbie stood a few yards off in an apparent daze. "We were so close," she said softly. "So close."

"You would never have made it to the settlements by yourselves," Nate responded. "I'm doing you a favor by escorting you back to your pa."

"If you only knew," she said.

Nate stared at Brian. Curled in a fetal position on the ground, the greenhorn was vigorously rubbing his eyes and whining pathetically. "I told you to stand," Nate declared, and delivered a light kick to the man's side. "You'd better listen. It wouldn't be wise to get me any madder than I am."

"Damn you!" Brian rasped, tears of anguish rolling down his cheeks. Lowering his hands, he pushed unsteadily to his feet. He cracked his eyelids, squinted at the world around him, and sniffled. "Lord, it hurts."

"But you can see, can't you?"

Brian glowered.

"Can't you?" Nate demanded, pointing a pistol at the greenhorn's midsection.

"Yes! No thanks to you!"

"Next time I'll slit your throat. Would that make you happier?" Nate said sarcastically, and moved closer to Libbie. "I'm disappointed in you," he informed her. "I thought we were friends."

"We are," she said.

"Then why did you help him?"

"I had to."

Why?"

She averted her gaze, her hands clasped at her waist, her shoulders trembling.

"Why?" Nate persisted.

"Leave her alone!" Brian declared, stepping nearer. "She's been tormented enough. But if you take her back, her torment will never end." He held out his hands as would a beggar desiring alms. "If you have a spark of decency in your soul, you'll forget this happened, mount up, and ride off."

"We're all going back," Nate said.

Brian drew himself up to his full height and opened his watery eyes a bit more. "The only way you're taking her back to that bastard is over my dead body."

"Don't tempt me."

"I mean it," Brian said, clenching his fists. "I don't care if you kill me. My life isn't important. Libbie's welfare is." He took a menacing stride. "So drop those pistols or else!"

"You're insane," Nate said, training both guns on the greenhorn's chest.

"I know what I'm doing," Brian stated gruffly. He took another pace. "What will it be, King? Do you allow us to leave, or will you have the murder of an innocent man on your conscience for the rest of your life?"

"I'm taking her to the wagons," Nate said, and cocked both flintlocks.

His eyes alight with passionate zeal, Brian paused and coiled to spring. "If not for your meddling, she would be safe right now. We'd be well on our way east. And Pudge, dear Pudge, would still be alive. He was the best friend I had in the whole world, and he died because of you."

"I had no part in his death. He was killed in the stampede. Those things happen all the time out here."

"Do they now?" Brian said bitterly. "But if you hadn't shown up at our camp when you did, if you hadn't delayed us further by attacking me when I went to shoot your horse, we wouldn't have been anywhere near that herd when they stampeded. We'd have been miles from the spot." He gazed sadly skyward and spoke to the clouds. "Why did it have to be Pudge? I saw that he was about to ride into a low limb and I yelled but he couldn't hear me. He went down and didn't move, and I had no chance to reach him before the bison did. I barely had time to get behind a boulder!"

There was no doubting the sincerity of the greenhorn's remorse, but Nate refused to accept responsibility for the tragedy. "If you're going to place blame, place some on yourself. If you hadn't spirited Libbie from her folks, *none* of this would have happened."

"I knew you wouldn't understand," Brian said, and unexpectedly leaped.

Nate was almost caught by surprise. Almost, yet not quite. He shifted to the right, so that Brian missed tackling him, and rammed a flintlock into the man's temple. Brian fell prone, stunned.

"No more!" Libbie screamed, dashing over and throwing herself protectively on top of the one she loved. "I can't stand to see him hurt! Please don't hit him again!"

"That's up to him."

She looked tenderly at the greenhorn, then caressed his brow. "You wouldn't despise him so if you knew the truth. And I think it's time you were told."

"No!" Brian blurted out in a whisper. "Don't!"

"Yes, beloved," Libbie said. "It's the only way. If he knows, he may agree to let us go."

"He has no right to know!" Brian disagreed. "It's our burden, and ours alone." Grunting, he rose on an elbow and raised his other hand to touch her cheek. "Let the past be buried. Every time you dig it up, every time you relive the nightmare, you're only adding to your misery."

"We *must*," Libbie insisted, and slowly rose to stare Nate straight in the eyes. "Mr. King, I don't blame you for any of this. You had no idea when you agreed to guide us that you would be working for a murderer."

"A murderer? Your father?"

Libbie nodded.

"Who did he kill?"

"Our child."

Nate glanced at Brian, who was as white as milk, then back at her. "I'll admit your father isn't the most tolerant man I've ever met, but a murderer? How do I know you're not making this up so I'll go along with what you want?"

"Not quite a year ago I gave birth to a healthy baby girl," Libbie disclosed, her lower lip quivering. "I'll admit I made a mistake. I should have waited to be in the family way until after Brian and I were married, but I couldn't help myself. I love him so much." She stopped, her voice breaking, and coughed. Do you have any idea how people in the States regard a woman who has a child out of wedlock, Mr. King?"

Nate nodded, but she seemed not to notice.

"They regard her as sinful. To them, she is no better than a common prostitute. People shun her. They go out of their way to avoid her. Even her church congregation wants nothing to do with her, and her family ends up sharing the blame," Libbie said, tears flowing freely. "I know. I saw it happen to a cousin of mine."

There was no need for words so Nate made no comment.

"I would have gladly faced all that," Libbie went on. "With Brian by my side, I would have faced anything. But my pa never liked Brian. Pa refused to let me see him, so I had to sneak away whenever I could." Her voice broke again. "When I became in the family way, Pa saw red. He beat me within an inch of my life, then vowed that no daughter of his was going to give the family a bad name by acting like a whore. He warned Brian to stay away from me or he would kill him. And he made me a prisoner in our own house. Once I was so big that it showed, he wouldn't even let me use the outhouse except at night."

Tears were pouring down Brian's face.

Libbie dabbed at the tip of her nose with her sleeve. "Ma helped me deliver, and as soon as the baby came out, Pa took her."

"Took her?" Nate repeated.

"Yes." Her tears were a virtual torrent now. "I never did find out where until a few months later when I came on a mound of dirt at the back of our property."

"Dear God."

"From then on, Pa wouldn't let me out of his sight. He was worried I'd soil the family name again. He was also scared someone might find out what had happened, so he decided we should move somewhere else and start all over. He sold our farm, and off to the promised land we went."

Nate let down the hammers on the flintlocks and tucked them under his belt. His throat was oddly constricted. There was also an itching sensation in his nose as he stepped up to her and put his hands on her slender shoulders. "You should have told me sooner."

"Now will you let us go in peace?"

"You'll never make it alone."

"We have to try."

"You don't have any guns. You don't have any supplies."

"We'll make do."

"And what about the hostiles? What about the grizzlies and all the other wild beasts?"

"God will watch over us."

The lump in Nate's throat grew, and he had to cough himself. "Why not go to Oregon? I'll make certain your pa doesn't bother you."

"We can't, and you know it."

"Then I'll find a spot in the hills where you can stay until I get back. I'll see you safely to Fort Leavenworth, and I won't charge you a penny."

Libbie smiled. "You're a kind man, Mr. King. I've always known that. But what about your family? And we both know Brian and I would be hard pressed to live off the land. We'd be better off heading east."

"There has to be another way."

"There isn't."

For all of ten seconds Nate racked his brain. At last, his soul heavy with sorry, his mind ablaze with indignation, he uttered a heartfelt, "Damn!" Then, again, so softly the word was barely audible. "Damn."

They saw him coming from a long way off, and were waiting in a state of nervous agitation when he reached the wagons. The Websters hung back. But Simon and Alice hurried up to him and the former gripped his arm as he dismounted.

"Speak, man! Where the devil is she? Don't tell me you couldn't find them?"

Nate stared at Banner's hand until the man removed it. Wearily, he tied Pegasus to a wheel and leaned back. "I found them, all right," he announced, "and I'm afraid I have bad news."

"Please, no" Alice breathed.

"You'll have to go on to the Oregon Territory by yourselves," Nate said.

"But what about Libbie?" Simon roared. "Is she alive? What could have happened to her and those two degenerates who took her?"

"The Piegans," Nate said.

Both husband and wife recoiled, aghast.

"Tell me it's not so!" Simon declared.

"I wish I could," Nate responded. "They ran into the rest of the same war party that attacked us."

For a fleeting second Simon's countenance reflected profound sorrow, then the sorrow was replaced by hate so overwhelming that he flushed scarlet and clenched his fists until the knuckles were pale. "It's all *their* fault! That sinful Derrick boy and his fat friend! They stole our precious girl out from under us and got her killed by their stupidity! If they were still alive I'd beat their brains out!" Spinning, he stalked off toward the stream, raining blows on everything in his path.

Nate watched him go, then looked at Alice. She was studying him from head to toe, her brow knit in deep thought.

"I've always taken you for a remarkably careful man, Mr. King. One of the most careful men I've ever met."

"Thank you."

"Yes indeed. So I find it quite surprising that you seem to have lost some of your effects while you were gone," Alice said, and pointed at his waist. "For instance, I could have sworn you once carried a knife with you."

"I dropped it somewhere."

"Oh. And did you also drop one of your pistols? I seem to recall you had two, not one."

"I lost it while going through thick brush. Don't fret yourself. I have another one at home."

"Thick brush, you say? Is that where you lost your powder horn and ammunition pouch as well?"

"I don't rightly know. It's not important. I have plenty to spare in my parfleche."

"Do you now?" Alice said, glancing at the stallion. "Why, you've apparently lost one of *those* as well. Didn't you have two before?"

"They never do stay on very well no matter how tight you tie them," Nate said.

Alice Banner's eyes were moist but sparkling with an inner light as she leaned forward and whispered, "Have no fear. Your secret is safe with me. I doubt my husband will even notice." Straightening, her cheeks and chin trembling she said huskily, "Bless you, sir. I only pray she finds the happiness she so truly deserves at long, long last."

"So do I, ma'am. More than you'll ever know."

Don't miss *Cheyenne #2: Death Chant!*
Available in November
at bookstores and newsstands
everywhere.

SPECIAL BONUS PREVIEW
FOLLOWS!

OUR STORY SO FAR...

Although still not accepted by Chief Yellow Bear's tribe, Touch the Sky continues his warrior training. But while off in the wilderness learning new skills, he and the other Indian youths stumble across a new threat to their people—and if they cannot stop it, innocent Cheyenne blood will turn the grassy plains red!

CHEYENNE #2: DEATH CHANT

Black Elk spotted something and knelt to examine the grassy bank of the river. Then he gathered the others around him and pointed to the tracks. "Iron hooves," he said. "White men's horses."

Black Elk showed them how to read the bend of the grass to tell how recent the tracks were. These were very fresh—the lush grass was still nearly pressed flat. A short distance along the bank, Touch the Sky and the others gaped in astonishment—the single set of tracks was joined by at least a dozen others!

They reached a huge dogleg bend in the river and worked their way through the thorny thickets in single file. The steady chuckle of the river helped to cover the sound of their passage. Touch the Sky emerged from the bend, following Little Horse, and cautiously poked his head around a hawthorn bush.

It took several long moments to understand what he was seeing. When the enormity of it finally sank in, he felt hot bile rise in his throat. Only a supreme effort kept him from retching.

The scene was a comfortable river camp. There were several pack mules, one of them asleep over its picket. The hindquarters of an elk bull hung high in a tree to protect it from predators. Buffalo robes and beaver pelts were heaped everywhere, pressed into flat packs for transporting. The air was sharp with the pungent smell of castoreum, the orange-brown secretion of the beaver. Touch the Sky knew it gave off a strong, wild odor and was used by trappers as a lure to set their traps.

But what made his gorge rise was the three naked, hideously slaughtered white men in the middle of the camp.

All three had been scalped. They had also been castrated and their genitals stuffed into their mouths. Their eyes had been gouged out and placed on nearby rocks, where they seemed to stare longingly at the bodies they had once belonged to.

The camp was crawling with living white men, who were heavily armed. The strings of their fringed buckskins had been blackened by constant exposure to the blood of dead animals. And while Touch the Sky watched, one of them knelt beside a fourth dead man. Expertly, he made a cut around the top of the dead man's head. Then he rose, one foot on his victim's neck, and violently jerked the bloody scalp loose.

Touch the Sky looked away when the man castrated the corpse and gouged his eyes out with the point of his knife. The buckskin-clad man worked casually, as if he were digging grubs out of old wood.

The man turned toward him and Touch the Sky took a good look. Some instinct warned him this was a face he should know. The man was tall and thickset, he wore his long, greasy hair tied in a knot. When he turned, Touch the Sky saw a deep, livid gash running from the corner of his left eye well past the corner of his mouth.

The huge man with the scar appeared to be in charge. Occasionally he barked an order that Touch the Sky could not hear from that range. Whoever and whatever these men were, this slaughter appeared to be all in a day's work to them. One of the men was calmly boiling a can of coffee and mixing meal with water to form little balls. He tossed them into the ashes to cook. The leader casually scooped a handful out of the ashes and munched on them while his other hand still held the dripping scalp.

He barked out another command, and another of his men began folding beaver traps and lashing them to a pack mule. Only then did Touch the Sky become aware of all the whiskey bottles scattered throughout camp. Spotting more unopened bottles in cases lashed to the mules, the youth realized what had probably happened. The murderers had made their victims stuporous with spirits, then killed them in their sleep.

The scene was so horrible that Touch the Sky nearly cried out when a hand fell on his shoulder. But it was only Little Horse, showing him that Black Elk was signalling the retreat.

"There are too many and they are well armed. We must return to Yellow Bear's camp at once and report this in council!" Black Elk said as soon as they were out of earshot. "I care nothing if the paleface devils slaughter one another. But I fear a great storm of trouble will come—these killings were done so as to seem that red men did them!"

CHEYENNE

Born Indian, raised white,
he'd die a free man!

#2: DEATH CHANT
by Judd Cole

When he left the home of his adopted parents and returned to his people, young Matthew Hanchon found that the Cheyenne could not fully trust anyone raised in the ways of the white man. Forced to prove his loyalty, Matthew faced the greatest challenge he had ever known. And when the death chant arose, Hanchon knew if he failed he would not die alone.

WATCH FOR OTHER ACTION-PACKED
CHEYENNE NOVELS—
COMING SOON TO BOOKSTORES AND
NEWSSTANDS EVERYWHERE.

__3337-2 $3.50 US/$4.50 CAN

LEISURE BOOKS
ATTN: Order Department
276 5th Avenue, New York, NY 10001

Please add $1.50 for shipping and handling for the first book and $.35 for each book thereafter. N.Y.S. and N.Y.C. residents, please add appropriate sales tax. No cash, stamps, or C.O.D.s. All orders shipped within 6 weeks via postal service book rate. Canadian orders require $2.00 extra postage. It must also be paid in U.S. dollars through a U.S. banking facility.

Name_____

Address_____

City _____ State_____ Zip_____

I have enclosed $_____in payment for the checked book(s).
Payment <u>must</u> accompany all orders.□ Please send a free catalog.